The Cowboy Meets His Match

MEAGAN McKINNEY

Published by Silhouette Books
America's Publisher of Contemporary Romance

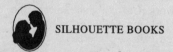

SILHOUETTE BOOKS

ISBN 0-373-76299-2

THE COWBOY MEETS HIS MATCH

Copyright © 2000 by Ruth Goodman

Printed in U.S.A.

Books by Meagan McKinney

Silhouette Desire

One Small Secret #1222
The Cowboy Meets His Match #1299

MEAGAN McKINNEY

is the author of over a dozen novels of hardcover and paperback historical and contemporary women's fiction. In addition to romance, she likes to inject mystery and thriller elements into her work. Currently she lives in the Garden District of New Orleans with her two young sons, two very self-entitled cats and a crazy red mutt. Her favorite hobbies are traveling to the Arctic and, of course, reading!

IT'S OUR 20th ANNIVERSARY!
We'll be celebrating all year,
Continuing with these fabulous titles,
On sale in June 2000.

One

"Jacquelyn, it's early Monday morning, and this is Hazel McCallum calling, dear. I have a...slightly unusual request to make of you. The last time you were here, it seems we got a bit sidetracked from your interview about Jake. It might be better if we meet at my home again. Please call at your convenience to arrange a time."

Jacquelyn Rousseaux hit the rewind button on the answering machine, feeling heat rise into her face.

Last time we got a bit sidetracked. My God, was that a polite understatement!

Jacquelyn still felt mortified for her uncharacteristic lack of restraint. Back in Atlanta, even those who had known her for years often learned little about her private life, yet, once she and Hazel had gotten to talking about life and hopes and dreams, she found she'd opened up like a floodgate to the older woman, who was practically a stranger. Jacquelyn had talked about the most personal and humiliating details of her life as if it were a catharsis.

She swept that unpleasant memory away, glancing at an old case clock in the back corner. It had kept near-perfect time in the office of the town's newspaper, the *Mystery Gazette,* since 1890.

Almost 10 a.m. She returned Hazel's call and quickly arranged to meet the Matriarch of Mystery, as Jacquelyn had secretly dubbed the famous cattle baroness, at 1 p.m. When she pressed Hazel for more information about that "slightly unusual request," the cagey old dame told her only, "You'll find out soon enough."

A pleasant-looking, middle-aged woman in a beige pantsuit stepped out of a Plexiglas cubicle at the front of the office. Managing Editor, Bonnie Lofton, held a pica pole in one hand, an X-Acto blade in the other. The *Gazette* was one of the last weekly newspapers in the country that was not computer composed. Bonnie laid out each offset-press page by hand for a distinctly "old-time" look, in the spirit of Mystery's upcoming sesquicentennial.

"Morning, Jacquelyn," Bonnie greeted her summer staffer. "Was that Hazel's voice I just heard?"

"None other. I already called her back. She wants to see me again. Won't tell me why, either. Not even a hint."

"Uh-huh, that's Hazel, all right. Sometimes she's Mystery's biggest mystery. Her heart's so generous, that woman won't let one person in this valley ever go cold or hungry. But she's the boss, and she expects everybody to know it."

"I hope it's not some problem with the last article I wrote," Jacquelyn said worriedly. "I verified all the quotes and double-checked the facts."

Bonnie gave a Gaelic wave of dismissal. "Oh, pouf! Are you kidding? You're the best feature writer we ever underpaid. I'll bet you anything your series on Jake McCallum ends up winning an award. Not even three years out of journalism school, and you already compose copy like a wire-service pro."

"Oh, right. I'll bet you say that to *all* the boss's kids."

Bonnie wagged the pica pole at her. ''Your old man's *not* the boss, kiddo, I am. He's the owner, by a quirk of corporate mergers, of this and a dozen other newspapers he probably doesn't ever read. I don't have to suck up to him *or* his kids. But face it, girl—you didn't have to come here and work for us, yet you've proven you're a journalist tried and true now. You're genuinely talented, and talent's a blessing nobody's money can buy.''

Jacquelyn smiled. She was pleased by Bonnie's firm but kind words. Bonnie, like many of the native Montanans Jacquelyn had met during her summer idylls in Mystery, was more reserved and private than folks back in Atlanta. Compliments were familiar verbal rituals in the South; out West, however, one earned and treasured them.

But talent, Jacquelyn thought with an inner stab of despair, is only one dimension of personality. For all her looks and education and ''correct upbringing,'' she was discovering it took more, so much more, to win at life—and love.

Joe's words came back to her, cruel and haunting, from that gray day in Atlanta. *I'm sorry, Jackie, but it's just not my fault you're solid ice from the neck down. Gina is everything you can't seem to be.*

With two brief sentences, her fiance left her for the woman she had trusted most. She suddenly felt a trembling heat behind her eyelids. For a panicky moment she feared she was going to lose it and cry right in front of her editor. With a superhuman effort she instead willed her face into a bright smile.

''Well, talent or no, Mystery's sesquicentennial has become Hazel's obsession. The last story I wrote on her great-grandfather Jake was reprinted upstate, and they got some dates mixed up. Hazel practically had a cow.''

Bonnie gave her a rueful grin. ''I can see why she's touchy about her family name. It will die with her, you know. That naturally makes her urgent to leave an accurate record.''

''The last McCallum,'' Jacquelyn said softly. ''I chickened

out when I tried to ask her why. I mean, I know her husband was killed in a car wreck near Lewistown when she was still young. But why didn't she remarry?''

Bonnie smiled. ''You may be smart as the dickens and pretty as four aces, but you still don't understand the essence of Hazel McCallum. The tougher Westerners are, the deeper they feel things. For women like Hazel, true love comes once, and it comes forever.''

Bonnie had only meant to explain, not wound. But Jacquelyn couldn't help filtering Bonnie's remark through the harsh lens of recent events back in Atlanta. Sure you've got brains and looks, Rousseaux, she told herself. But you're an ice princess—so much of one that your own boyfriend dumped you for your own so-called best friend.

Bonnie seemed to note the shadow that crossed her face. ''Open mouth, insert foot,'' Bonnie apologized, touching Jacquelyn's shoulder in a gesture of sympathy. ''I'm sorry, hon. Look, I'm all caught up on my work right now. Wanna have a cup of coffee and just shoot the breeze?''

In her secret heart of hearts, Jacquelyn welcomed Bonnie's attempt at friendship. For years she had sensed a ''secret self'' within her who was desperately yearning to thaw those layers of ice. But that secret self simply was not strong enough to endure the brutal slings and arrows of romantic fortune.

Joe and Gina had hurt her at the very core of her being, had shaken not only her world but her very soul. And the only way Jacquelyn knew how to deal with such trauma was to cover it over with a layer of frost—numbing it, yes, but also leaving it fully intact. That's precisely how Stephanie Rousseaux had taught her daughter to cope—as she herself endured a loveless marriage to Jacquelyn's cruel, critical father.

So even as her heart secretly responded to Bonnie's warmth, Jacquelyn knew her survival reflexes would chill the woman out.

"Thanks, Bonnie, but I'd better not. If I'm going to make the Wednesday deadline with this next installment, I'd better get to work."

"Okay, busy lady. But the offer's open."

Bonnie watched her from concerned eyes. Then she added, "You know what else? When he was young, my grandpa rode for Jake McCallum on the Lazy M spread. Every man who rode for Jake could quote the old man's favorite saying. 'The best way to cure a boil is to lance it.'"

"All right, then, A.J.," Hazel confirmed, "I'll see you around, say, two o'clock this afternoon at my place? Good. I can always count on you Clayburn men, can't I? It shouldn't take too long."

Hazel still used the stodgy, old black phones from the fifties. She hung the handset back in its cradle, a determined smile smoothing out the lines around her mouth.

She strolled, still lost in thought, toward a big bay window in the parlor's north wall. At seventy-five, she considered herself still young. Every morning she arose, twisted her long, white hair into the ever-present chignon at the back of her neck and got going, running the enormous ranch from her cell phone and Jake's original rolltop desk. She was still quite active, too, though a long succession of cattle-country winters had left her "a little rusted in the hinges," as she often said, dismissing the arthritis in her joints.

There was still a lot of life in her that she meant to live. But...

Halting in the window bay, she parted the curtains and the lace liners with both hands to gaze outside. Beyond the hay-raked pastures of the Lazy M, ragged tatters of cloud drifted across a late-morning sky the pure blue color of a gas flame. The lower slopes of the mountains surrounding Mystery Valley bristled with conifers and white sycamores. Higher up, the slopes were wooded only in the gulches, rising in ascending folds to granite points draped in white ermine.

Looking at the familiar yet still-stunning view made Hazel think about Jacquelyn Rousseaux and the conversation they'd had during her interview.

The girl had admitted being hurt, betrayed, deeply disillusioned. She honestly believed that love had given her the permanent go-by. Hazel had seen all that when Jacquelyn opened up to her last week. But Hazel also recognized how deeply, how desperately the young woman wanted to believe again in the old dreams, the "corny" ideals about love, men and life.

Toward that very end, among others, Hazel had a plan. She wanted, more than anything else, to see Mystery go on being the kind of town it was always meant to be. Rodeo star and dear family friend, A. J. Clayburn, fit the bill exactly; he'd been out to stud for too many years without marrying and settling down. Hazel knew full well why the cowboy's heart was frozen, but when Jacquelyn Rousseaux began to open up to her in the interview, Hazel realized it was time the cowboy's heart got to melting. And she'd sat looking at the cool, platinum-haired beauty who was just the one to do it.

The time was right. Hazel wasn't getting any younger or more energetic. And she had to face the hard facts: she was the last McCallum, and she would leave no line behind her. Only one thing could keep Mystery from obliteration under an influx of careless investors and outsiders like Jacquelyn's father, the developer Eric Rousseaux: new blood had to be carefully, *passionately* mixed with old. She meant to create new families from the ones already committed to the town.

Simply put, she had made a list of good folks in Mystery who needed hitching up. Despite being long past retirement age, Hazel, matriarch of all the land as far as the eye could see, was now taking on a second career—matchmaking. And one of her first clients was none other than the troubled beauty who wrote for the town newspaper.

Still, Hazel fretted about the prospects for success in Jacquelyn's case. If someone wanted to know how a young woman might likely turn out in life, they had only to look at her mother. And Hazel had seen the abject hopelessness in the eyes of Stephanie Rousseaux, who summered in Mystery with Jacquelyn. Not exactly the ideal role model for a daughter reeling from emotional disaster.

But the plan was much bigger than Jacquelyn Rousseaux, even though it began with her. Hazel's fires might be banked, but not her big ambition. Her idea, in fact, was literally as big as an entire town.

Again her Prussian-blue eyes sought those majestic white peaks on the horizon. For her plan to work, Hazel needed women to match those mountains. Strong, beautiful, proud, enduring women. Women just like Jacquelyn Rousseaux, broken heart, Southern drawl, disillusionment and all.

Or am I wrong this time, Hazel wondered. Mistaking hope for reality, a plow horse for a racer?

She would find out in about three hours, when Jacquelyn finally understood what the older woman expected her to do.

Two

"Jake wasn't an educated man," Hazel confided to Jacquelyn. "Swore like a trooper, when he *thought* there were no women or children nearby to hear him. Used to joke that he spoke only two languages—American and cussing. But he sure did have what they call money smarts."

The two women sat near each other in the parlor's nineteenth-century gilt chairs. Jacquelyn's microcassette recorder included a tiny but powerful high-ambience remote microphone, so she could tape Hazel without rudely shoving anything into her face.

"Before he died," Hazel resumed, "Jake even became part owner in the Comstock Lode. That was a rich deposit of silver and gold ore discovered by his old partner, Henry T. P. Comstock, near Virginia City, Nevada. Jake's side ventures eventually allowed my grandpa to be the first cattleman in these northern ranges to develop Shorthorn and Hereford breeds. Better meat than the Longhorn stock from the Texas ranges. Sold higher, too."

While Hazel spoke, Jacquelyn again admired Mystery Valley's oldest and still finest ranch house. Built in the 1880s, it had replaced the original settlers' cabin.

Its hand-hewn hemlock beams had been transported cross-country by cumbersome freight wagons. Other materials, too, had been selected to reflect success, not frontier frugality: a carved cherrywood staircase, hard-maple flooring, fireplaces manteled with blood onyx, marble and slate. On the wall behind Hazel, bright buffalo-hide shields flanked a beautiful wash drawing in a gold scrollwork frame. It depicted a small herd of Shorthorns splashing across a river, whipping the water to spray.

"Jake was a tough man," Hazel reminisced in her deep, still-vibrant voice. "He insisted that all his children be educated, even his daughters, which was unusual in his day. That included my grandma, his daughter Mystery."

Hazel fell silent, thoughtfully studying her young interviewer.

Jacquelyn felt as if she towered over the petite older woman, even seated, though she was only five-four. She waited for the next goldmine of information and was embarrassed to find the conversation again focused on her.

"You know I don't cotton to short hair on women, but I think I like yours. In my day we'd call your hair color platinum. Marilyn-Monroe platinum. Quite glamorous. And I do believe your eyes are sea-green, aren't they?"

Puzzled at the inspection, Jacquelyn quickly thumbed off the recorder. Something in the old girl's determined visage signaled that the interview part of the visit was over. She supposed they were going to get around to the "slightly unusual request."

"You know, Jacquelyn, at my age a woman can't help warming her hands at the fire of the past. But while we should always recall our dead, this world belongs to the living."

Jacquelyn raised an interrogatory eyebrow, waiting for more. "Yes?" she encouraged.

But Hazel kept her waiting, as if she was mulling possible explanations for the old matriarch's secret.

Finally she said, "You told me last time that you want to capture the true feel of Jake's pioneer experience, remember?"

"Of course. I *hoped* my articles were doing that."

"Your articles are wonderful, dear. Quite honestly, I expected the usual twaddle and bunkum about grizzled pioneers. But you've captured the essence of Jake McCallum better than any other writer who's tried. And many have."

Hazel snatched up a copy of last week's *Mystery Gazette* from a pedestal stand beside her chair.

"'Jake McCallum,'" she read out loud, "'was a man who went a great distance while others were still debating whether to leave today or tomorrow.'"

The corners of her eyes crinkled deeply when Hazel laughed. "Jacquelyn, you *do* understand that old rascal's basic nature. But for your own sake I want you to go that great distance, too. Or at least part of it. The important part."

"I'm sorry, I don't understand."

"I'd like you to actually repeat Jake's original journey. Not the entire trip, of course. As you already know, his original plan was to travel from his home in St. Louis all the way north to the Yukon to mine for gold."

Jacquelyn smiled. "Yes. Until he was waylaid in a beautiful Montana valley to help a rancher with some straying cattle, right?"

"Right as rain. Because that rancher had a pretty daughter of marrying age named Libbie. One look at her, and Jake wrote back home that he was settling in Montana. The part of his journey that Jake's journal mentions most was the hard, but beautiful, five-day ride through the mountains and Eagle Pass to this valley. Called McCallum's Trace to this day."

"And that's the part of the journey you'd like me to

make?'' Jacquelyn mulled the odd suggestion for a few moments. Well, so what if it was a bit…eccentric of Hazel to suggest it? After all, Jacquelyn didn't want to be one of those journalists who never left the office to find a story. And it really was an important piece of American history.

"All right," she finally agreed, her face brightening. "It sounds like fun. My family has a Hummer at the summer lodge here that usually just sits in the garage. I'll borrow it. I could also—what?"

She broke off, confused at the way Hazel was shaking her head to silence her.

"Jacquelyn, we're talking about the 'true feel,' remember? Your own words. My lands, Jake didn't cross those high-altitude passes in a Hummer—nor was there a highway, just an old Sioux Indian game trail. That's still all there is up there.''

Jacquelyn's jaw dropped slightly, and her eyes widened. "Hazel. You want me to *ride* across the original trace? Five days on horseback?"

"Well, you do ride, don't you? I've seen you in your fancy riding britches. And there's horses at your place."

"Well…yes, I ride. But—"

Hazel dismissed her objections with a careless wave. "I rode that trail myself when I was about your age. Never in winter, of course, as Jake did. In August, just like you'll be doing. Gets a bit nippy at night, especially up in Eagle Pass. Sure, you might even see some snow, but it's quite exhilarating."

"Hazel, you simply don't understand. I ride, yes. But it's the English style I learned at boarding school. You know—dressage, preparation for show jumping, things like disciplined turns and reverses, fancy jumps and tricky hurdles. Not trail riding in rugged mountains. Hazel, I—that is, I've never even been a Girl Scout. I wouldn't know the most basic—"

"Oh, all your objections are just pee doodles," Hazel

scoffed, her eyes cutting to an ormolu clock on the mantel. "Because you're going to have the perfect guide for this little trek."

"Guide?" Jacquelyn repeated, immediately feeling like a parrot.

"I should say! None other than Mystery's own world-champion saddle-bronc rider, A. J. Clayburn."

Hazel opened up a photo album lying on the pedestal table and passed it over to her visitor. "This is A. J. at the rodeo at the Calgary Stampede, accepting his World Cup. One of the proudest days in Mystery's recent memory."

Jacquelyn took in gunmetal-blue eyes as direct as a Remington, an unruly thatch of thick, brown hair that touched his collar. The scornful twist to the mouth irritated her immediately. The handsome man in this photo radiated the easy calm and confidence, bordering on arrogance, of men who were good at handling animals—and thought the talent translated to women, as well.

"You've seen him around town, no doubt?" Hazel inquired.

Jacquelyn nodded, still too numb and confused by all this to speak. She had seen him around town, all right. How could anyone miss those metallic eyes and his wide-shouldered, slim-hipped frame? A. J. Clayburn was straight off the cover of a Western novel—but whether the hero or the bad guy, she wasn't sure. Still, there was no mistaking the living, breathing personification of a great American myth.

But there was no way Hazel could expect her to travel McCallum's Trace with this man. It was like putting a duck in the desert. He was utterly foreign to Jacquelyn's genteel, urban world, and vice versa.

Hazel seemed to read some of these thoughts in her visitor's stunned face.

"Believe me, honey," she assured, taking the photo album back from her. "You'll quickly learn to appreciate A.J.'s qualities. He's what we Western gals like to call an 'unflighty' man. Nowadays, of course, that's not what it once was. I don't recall any flighty men who took Omaha Beach.''

"Hazel, I just don't think—''

"Generally,'' Hazel nattered on blithely, cutting her off, "when he's not on the rodeo circuit, you'll find A.J. perched on the top board of a corral somewhere in the valley.''

"Hazel, honestly, I can't see me—''

"But he's not riding this season, you understand. At the year's first rodeo in Miles City, A.J. caught his spur in a cinch. The horse went over on his leg and crushed it. Now he's knitting, but it was a bad fall. It's not clear if the doctors will certify him for the circuit again. Leaves A.J. with some free time to take on guide jobs for me.''

"I'm sorry he's had an accident. But—''

"Not that he's pining away and burning any daylight,'' Hazel charged on. "Lands no! A.J. stays busy—a little too busy, if you catch my meaning.'' She winked. "He's left a mighty long trail of broken hearts, but still I remember his ma and pa. They were something fierce in love. The kind you don't see nowadays. A love like the kind I had.'' Hazel smiled at her. "Oh, he'll have a love like that one day. It's just taken him a while to come around. In the meantime, while his leg's been healing, he's helping out his old partner Cas Davis. Cas runs a popular rodeo-riding school in Thompson Falls.''

Hazel finally paused to take a breath.

"I can't do this,'' Jacquelyn blurted out. "I'm sorry. Not only am I unprepared for the ride, but A. J. Clayburn is a stranger to me. I can't just go camping in the wilderness—''

"He won't be a stranger in a few minutes,'' Hazel assured her, again glancing at the clock. "A.J. will be here any moment now to meet you.''

For a short, panicked moment, Jacquelyn felt her breath catch.

"Meet me?'' she repeated foolishly, stunned at this massive loss of control in her very controlled life. *Am I a mail-order bride?* she almost asked in disbelief.

"Since you'll be spending so much time alone with A.J.," Hazel added, "I suppose I should also mention that he has a recently acquired police record."

Jacquelyn could feel the blood drain from her cheeks. Hazel laughed.

"Steady, dear. He *can* be rehabilitated. I'm quite sure of it. You've heard of Red Lodge, Montana?"

Still shell-shocked, Jacquelyn answered woodenly. "The town where cowboys and rodeo types rendezvous every Fourth of July for a party, right?"

"I suppose you could call that annual riot a party. Anyhow, this year A.J. was arrested for riding his horse into the Snag Bar saloon. Evidently, a deputy or two 'accidentally ran their jaws into my fist,' as A.J. put it in court."

Oh, great, Jacquelyn thought, her stomach sinking. So he's a drunken brawler, too? How lucky can one woman get?

"If you *really* want the true feel of being with Jake McCallum and along on his ride," Hazel told the reporter, "you couldn't be with a more similar man. Just as Jake was, A.J. is fast out of the gate."

Hazel laughed at the alarm that must have flickered in Jacquelyn's eyes.

"Dear, relax. It's just an old saying. Means a man is clear about what he wants and how to get it. Tell me…is it your skin you're fretting about?"

"My…skin?"

"I've always been told you Southern women take special pride in your beautiful complexions. You're living proof of that."

"Thank you," she said politely, but it was obvious that Hazel was only jabbering like this to head off any more objections about her wild idea.

She was on the verge of demanding *why* it was so important that she make this mountain trek. But just then a two-tone chime sounded within the parlor. Nervous fear made her heart speed up for the next few beats.

"That will be A.J.," Hazel announced with evident satisfaction. "Donna will let him in."

The tap of solid boot heels reached their ears as the new arrival moved through the kitchen and dining room. Jacquelyn's trapped-deer desperation didn't seem to escape Hazel's notice—or her sympathy.

"Everything will be just fine, dear, I promise. I won't sugarcoat the dangers of those mountains. But with a guide like A. J. Clayburn, you'll be fine."

"But I really don't understand why this is necessary. You said you liked my articles—that they were authentic," Jacquelyn whispered in a rush to beat the footsteps. "Why is this so important? Why?"

Something secret and mysterious glinted in Hazel's eyes—something born of great ambition, great determination and great love. But her evasive answer only further frustrated Jacquelyn.

"Be patient. Making this journey will change your life, I assure you. Very few have taken it. Well, would you look who's here, Jacquelyn! Timely, yet! Well, my land, A.J., don't just stand there gawking, come on in. She doesn't bite!"

Three

Jacquelyn paid scant attention as Hazel went through the formalities of introducing her to Mystery's leading rodeo celebrity.

Besides feeling confused, trapped and manipulated, she was almost indignant. Somehow she felt she was being hazed, as cowboys called it when they forced cattle to move where they wanted them to go.

Or more like it, Jacquelyn punned wryly to herself, she was being Hazeled.

"Personally," Hazel nattered while Jacquelyn gathered her composure a bit, "I've become a dyed-in-the-wool homebody in my old age. I subscribe to the theory that a gal should never leave her time zone. But then, if some of us didn't travel, we wouldn't have Jacquelyn here summering with us in Mystery, would we, A.J.?"

"I guess that's so," the cowboy agreed reluctantly. His tone made it clear he could survive that contingency just fine.

He sat across from the two women in a leather wing chair,

an immaculate gray Stetson balanced on his left knee. He wore clean range clothes and a neckerchief. Long, muscular, blue-jeans-clad legs were tucked into hand-stitched, high-heeled boots so pointy they looked like weapons. A. J. Clayburn, Jacquelyn noted reluctantly in a brief appraisal, was every bit as handsome as the photo of him in Hazel's album.

But, in person, he also projected a sense of...physical readiness—even danger. That was undeniable even though he walked a bit stiff-legged from his recent injury.

Also undeniable was his smug awareness of his own abilities. He certainly would not shine among the old, genteel social circles back in Atlanta's Peachtree Park, where subtlety and nuance opened doors of opportunity. But Jacquelyn had to grudgingly admit he was the kind of man she would want nearby in a crisis. Though, God knows, she'd want him gone after the trouble was over. *Immediately* after.

"If you youngsters will excuse me," Hazel said, rising spryly from her chair, "I need to go upstairs and find some old letters that Jacquelyn requested for her series. You two will want to get acquainted, of course, and discuss your arrangements. I'll try not to be too long."

Again Jacquelyn felt dismay pulsing in her temples. *Arrangements?* Hazel was simply taking over her life, to hell with permission. And now came the lame pretext—she was leaving Jacquelyn virtually trapped with this arrogant, self-inflated rube.

A.J. rose politely while Hazel stood and left the parlor. So far, while Hazel was present, he had spared Jacquelyn the force of those penetrating eyes of his. Indeed, each time his gunmetal gaze touched her it slid quickly away.

As if he resented her presence.

Now that they were alone, however, all that changed. Jacquelyn felt his eyes on her, so probing and intense she felt violated by them.

"Is there a fly on my nose?" she finally asked, heat flooding into her face.

"Nope. Just looking."

"It's just looking, maybe, for the first few seconds. But eventually it becomes staring."

His sardonic mouth twisted into a grin. "'At's funny."

"It is?"

"You don't *look* like a book. But you sure-god talk like one."

"Pardon me." She commented, "I'll try to sound more obtuse so you won't feel challenged."

Her acerbic tone didn't daunt him at all; probably because he didn't get the insult. She ached to dismiss him, but beneath his continued scrutiny she felt a flush heat her skin. Nervously she stood up and quickly smoothed her black matte jersey skirt over her thighs. Then she crossed to the wall behind her, covered with paintings and photographs. She could still feel the almost physical force of his stare.

"Mr. Clayburn, Hazel has told me her plan, but I'm afraid I'm not a camper, nor a horse packer. It seems she thinks I'm the best one to write about McCallum Trace, but there's a fine young college boy interning at the office, and I think he'd be a much more appropriate choice for your—"

"You don't have to convince me. I'm Mohammed. I can come to the mountain myself." He jerked his head toward the door where Hazel had gone. "It's the mountain you got to worry about moving."

Jacquelyn looked at the empty doorway. The sinking feeling betrayed her cold bravado. The cowboy was, unfortunately, right; truer words and all that. Hazel *was* the mountain, and Jacquelyn Rousseaux might have an Ivy League education and a trust fund which she eschewed in order to make her own money and be her own woman, but she did not possess a backhoe.

So in the end her battle was with Hazel, not the man stuck in the room with her. Her innate Southern politeness finally won out.

"So...I understand you're a rodeo champ," she said, going back to her seat to wait for Hazel.

"That's old news around here. Heard anything more interesting?"

His insolent, taunting tone made her want to spar with him. Worse was the strange feeling she had whenever his gaze raked over her. She realized she must have been far too long without male companionship because his every glance, his every stare was making her feel exposed and strangely flustered.

"You writing about cowboys, too?" he asked.

In spite of her better judgment, she retorted, "Actually I was thinking about it." Archly she said, "In researching my articles on Jake McCallum, I read something about Montana cowboys. Is it true y'all are defensive because you're just imitations of the true Texas cowboys?"

"'Y'all?'" he repeated, raising one eyebrow.

To her chagrin he was unruffled. Then, to her surprise, he had managed to turn the question to her.

And Hazel seriously thought Jacquelyn would spend five days—not to mention nights—alone with this insulting, boorish hick?

There was no use in continuing the small talk. She turned her attention to an old, nineteenth-century tintype photo of Hazel's grandmother, Mystery McCallum. Mystery wore a swag-fronted, bustled gown and a tight-laced corset to give her the wasp waist that had been fashionable then.

When A.J. spoke, his voice was so close to her ear that Jacquelyn almost flinched.

"I've heard that all those tight lacings sometimes kindled 'impure desires.' You being female and all, tell me—is that possible, you think?"

She spun around to face him, stepping back away from his invasion of her personal space. But not before she caught the scent of him—a decidedly masculine aroma of good leather and bay rum aftershave. The smell made her stomach quiver, as if it had some kind of hormonal effect on her, as if it kind of…kind of…turned her on.

She took a step backward and vowed to get out more and meet men now that she was unattached again. In her deprivation she was becoming a little too worked up about nothing. Certainly rawhide and dimestore aftershave weren't her perferred sexual stimulants.

But then she caught another whiff of it, and she wondered if he wasn't getting the best of her without even trying. Only pride stopped her from running from the room in terror, her nose pinched to protect her from her own unwanted chemical reactions.

With great effort she tossed him a bored, dismissive glance. "I'm so sorry. Did you say something?"

His handsome mouth twisted in a grin. "I don't believe I whispered. I was asking you about corsets."

"Well, I'm sorry to ruin your bunkhouse fantasies, but I don't wear a corset and never have. But what I know from history is that tight corsets cracked ribs and deformed internal organs. They also constricted breathing and blood flow. I'm sure that's obvious from the pictures, and I hardly think any of it was a thrill."

"You've researched that, too—along with cowboys, huh, ice princess?"

It was only one silly insult among others he had already heaped on her in a brief time. But his remark cut dangerously close to memories that were still like open wounds. *It's not my fault you're solid ice from the neck down.*

For a second the old pain and humiliation rushed back, so fresh it numbed her. All over again she felt like one of those sordid, vulgar, shouting idiots on the tabloid TV shows— betrayed and publicly mortified by the very people she counted on most to sympathize with her.

The cowboy stood only a few feet away. His gleaming, invasive gaze held her while he waited for her to reply.

Hazel saved the day by arriving at the awful moment. She

bustled into the parlor, skirts rustling, carrying an old-fashioned musette bag stuffed with faded envelopes.

"Here you go, Jacquelyn, some of Jake's letters from the folks back East. I trust you two had a chance to discuss your upcoming ride?"

Jacquelyn had to fight to slow her pounding heart. It was now or never.

"Hazel, I can't go," she managed to say, with great difficulty, accepting the letters from Hazel. She hurried back to her chair to retrieve her recorder. Then she headed toward the wide parlor doors. During all the fluster of activity she refused to look in Clayburn's direction.

"I'm sorry, Hazel, but it's simply out of the question. I...I just can't. I'm sorry."

"All right, dear," Hazel said, dismissing her. "It's my fault, I suppose, for jumping to conclusions. One can't assume the wood is solid just because the paint is pretty."

"Yeah, she looks that way all right," A.J.'s voice added behind Jacquelyn. "You ask me, though, the whole dang Rousseaux family needs to move their summer lodge out of here. They'd be more at home in a sunny condo in Florida or California. Among their own kind."

Jacquelyn had been on the feather edge of rushing from the house, but Clayburn's words acted on her like a brake. She turned to stare at him.

"And just what kind might that be, Mr. Clayburn?" she demanded, convinced her green eyes were snapping sparks.

"The grasping kind," he told her bluntly and without hesitation. "I know all about your father and his dang plans to develop and ruin Mystery Valley. I'm no fan, Miss Rousseaux. I have no need for big-city developers and jet-setting money-grubbers who get rich off other men's risk and labor. So what kind, Miss Rousseaux? The carpetbagging, uppity, Perrier-sipping, spoiled-brat kind who need to be brought down to size. *That* kind, Miss Rousseaux."

He hurled each word at her like a poison-tipped spear.

But Jacquelyn only became even more determined and defiant. "I'll have you know, Mr. Clayburn, that I don't support my father in his company's demand to develop Mystery Valley. But I'll remind you that it's not your place nor my place to make that decision for this community. It's up to the town council to vote on it. And if you have an opinion, Mr. Rodeo Star, why don't you hire someone to write it down for you and exercise your rights in this democracy of ours and give it to your town council."

The silence almost boomed after she was through.

Hazel watched them both with the rapture of a tennis fan at Forest Hills.

Then suddenly A. J. Clayburn broke out in rude, lustful laughter. "I'll be damned. You must be a writer. Nobody else I know could do that in a paragraph the way you just did."

The anger almost choked her. "You know very well I'm a journalist, and it was not given to me, by the way, Mr. Clayburn. I had to work hard at it."

"Even if Daddy does own the paper," he taunted, his steely gaze shadowed by the rim of his hat.

"Even if Daddy does own the paper," she defied, pronouncing every cold word.

"Then I'm half sorry we're not going up on that mountain, miss. Maybe you could teach me a new word or two." He looked at Hazel, resignation in his handsome smile.

"Hazel, I've changed my mind," Jacquelyn announced, surprising even herself. "Mr. Clayburn, Hazel has my work and home phone numbers. Since we'll be crossing one of the most difficult mountain passes in the Continental Divide, would I be *too* much of an 'uppity, Perrier-sipping brat' if I request at least one day to prepare?"

"You go right ahead, Miss Rousseaux. Do whatever you think is necessary," he said as if patronizing her.

Hazel walked her out, looking way too pleased by Jacquelyn's anger. Just as she was about to let the younger woman through the front door, Hazel whispered, "Don't you worry about anything on the trip, Jacquelyn. A.J. will handle it. That's why he's the best one to take you. Oh, and by the way, don't go teaching him any new words, either." The older woman gave a meaningful pause. "He'd only want to learn the dirty Latin ones, anyway."

Hazel's Lazy M spread sat in the exact center of verdant Mystery Valley. Several thousand acres of lush pasture criss-crossed by creeks and run-off streams and dotted with scarlet patches of Indian paintbrush.

The town of Mystery, with a year-round population of four thousand, was a pleasant fifteen-minute drive due east from the Lazy M's stone gateposts. The Rousseaux's summer lodge was a ten-minute walk to the west, the ranch's nearest habitation.

Jacquelyn, who had driven to Hazel's place from the *Gazette* offices, turned east out of Hazel's long driveway. Her thoughts, like her emotions, were still in a confused riot. *What* had she just committed herself to? How could she possibly ever endure such an ordeal—especially in the company of such a man?

Tears abruptly filmed her eyes. The extent of her vulnerability surprised and dismayed her. A. J. Clayburn's crude baiting had brought back all the insecurities, all the bitter misery Joe and Gina had dragged her through.

Gina and Joe had proved perfect for each other, a matched set. As harmonious as the easy, breezy alliteration of their names. They were both charming, careless people, takers not givers, and honored no laws except self-survival and gratification of their sensual pleasures. And they had taught her a valuable lesson: it was easier to deal with known enemies than with phony friends.

At least, she had to admit as she reached the outskirts of town, A. J. Clayburn wasn't feigning friendship.

She parked her car. When she entered the office, the red

light was on over the darkroom door, which meant Bonnie was busy making photo-offset plates for the next issue of the paper. She left a brief note explaining Hazel's imperious request, then hung up her hat for the day.

She was returning to her BMW, angle parked out front, when a throaty female voice cut into the tumult of her thoughts.

"Hey, there! How's 'bout a ride for an old geezer?"

Jacquelyn saw her mother veer toward her along the brick sidewalk, carrying a plastic shopping bag. It bulged from the weight of several clinking liquor bottles.

"I walked to town," Stephanie Rousseaux explained, "with all sorts of healthy aerobic intentions. But next time I get the fitness urge, I'll remember to wear tennis shoes. Good God, my feet are killing me! I can't wait until your father and I return to Atlanta. How I wish at least one of our local rednecks would exchange his pickup truck for a limo service."

At forty-eight, Stephanie was still a striking woman, her hair covering the right side of her face in a hip style. Though lately she was stouter than she had been and a bit more grim around the mouth. She made it a point of honor to always be civil and even-tempered. But while she was far too cultivated and controlled to ever create an emotional scene, Stephanie had developed a chilly, disengaged manner that stymied others around her. Including her own daughter.

"Some of the local yokels," Stephanie remarked as her daughter backed out into the sparse traffic of Main Street, "seem surprised that I'm still sober at midday."

"Mother," Jacquelyn pleaded, "please don't start with that."

"Start with what, Miss Goody Two-shoes?" Stephanie countered, adjusting her diva shades. "I'm quite proud that I have strict rules concerning my addiction. I'm disciplined, just like your dear old dad. After all, baby, decorum should rule everything, don't you agree? Even a Southern debutante's failed life.''

Mine or yours? Jacquelyn felt like shouting. But there was no point. She knew her mother meant herself.

"You know," Jacquelyn said, keeping her tone patient and persuasive, "they have A.A. meetings out here, too, Mom. I checked it out. And you know, Dr. Rendquist told you—''

"Zip it. Renquist doesn't know his elbow from his libido. The only reason I go to him is because he keeps me in touch with the charming Prince Valium. I've decided A.A. is for the great unwashed masses. Your elitist mother has a better system.''

Stephanie shook the bag, clinking the glass bottles inside to emphasize her point.

"Discipline. No therapy until the sun goes down. I despise a daylight drunk. Those lushes at A.A. lack discretion, self-control.''

Discretion and self-control. Two traits instilled in Stephanie back in Queen Anne County, by parents whose ancestry traced back to the First Families of Virginia. Traits that had proven invaluable for surviving a loveless marriage to a faithless, hypercritical man.

Jacquelyn ached to say something that might break through to her mother's inner core. She knew, from her own childhood memory of her mother, that she had once possessed a deep well of inner feeling. But that well had long since gone dry.

Jacquelyn had borne silent witness for many years. By now Stephanie Rousseaux merely went through the motions of living. She simply reminded herself to change her facial expression now and then, so people would think she was properly "involved." But in fact her existence had become a long, unbroken silence—the empty and meaningless stillness left behind when love and hope are abandoned.

And there was nothing her daughter could tell her to make things different. Stephanie was the frost queen Jacquelyn feared she herself was becoming—had perhaps already become. A chip off the old ice block.

Now Jacquelyn watched the town of Mystery roll past the car windows, alone with her thoughts. Downtown Mystery still included plenty of its original red brick buildings with black iron shutters—nothing fancy, just practical and sturdy. But the ornate, nineteenth century opera house with its scrollwork dome still placed the community a cut above plain saloon towns. So did the stately old courthouse, the only gray masonry building in town.

"Not exactly the height of sartorial splendor or exotic cuisine," Stephanie drawled in her droll, husky voice. "But no squalid industrial sprawls, either. Although your father is working on that as I speak—that is, unless he's relieving his stress with one of his new consultants."

Consultants. The euphemism of choice, Jacquelyn realized, to designate the string of mistresses that Eric Rousseaux seemed to require in order to "validate his manhood."

Hazel's Lazy M Ranch slid by on their left as Jacquelyn headed toward the Rousseaux's summer lodge at the western edge of Mystery Valley. A. J. Clayburn's old rattletrap pickup truck was just at the entrance, turning to town. He passed them, tipping his hat while he went. Jacquelyn wondered if he recognized her car, or if he was just the good-ol'-boy type who tipped his hat to everyone in his path.

Again cold dread filled her limbs as if they were buckets under a tap. She wondered again what she had agreed to.

The Rousseaux place sat in a little teacup-shaped hollow about three-quarters of a mile west of the Lazy M. It was surrounded by bottom woods and Hazel's pastures on the east and south, jagged mountains to the north and west.

The sprawling two-storey lodge was made of redwood timbers with a cedar-shake roof. Out back was the lodge guest house that Jacquelyn—insisting on independence—rented from her father. Additionally, there was a big pole corral, and low stables sported a fresh coat of white paint. Jacquelyn liked the lodge's proximity to town. Often she had time to ride Boots, her big sorrel thoroughbred, into Mystery instead of driving. Though her mother and father both kept horses, too, neither of them rode much anymore.

Jacquelyn parked in the paved stone driveway out front.

"Home sweet home," Stephanie said with lilting irony. "Thanks for the ride, kiddo."

Jacquelyn headed through the house instead of around while Stephanie took her purchases into the basement to re-stock the wet bar. Jacquelyn encountered her father on the phone in the living room.

At fifty-one, Eric Rousseaux was trim and athletic—one of those vain middle-aged men who constantly found excuses to remove his shirt so others could admire the hard slabs of his sculpted abs and pecs.

He had accumulated his considerable fortune in newspaper publishing. Eric owned controlling interest in several major daily newspapers and a handful of smaller weeklies. Including, by monopolistic takeover, the *Mystery Gazette*. Recently, however, he had diversified into land-site development ventures.

"Money," her father had once solemnly informed her, using the old cliché, "is like manure. It has to be spread around."

Eric tossed his daughter a careless wave as she entered the room. Before she could hear what he was saying, he backed into his den and closed the door with his heel—talking in private on the phone was something he did a lot these days.

Was "the Lothario of the ink-slinging industry," as her mother called him, involved in yet another romantic intrigue? Stephanie's liquor consumption lately suggested he was.

A hopeless weight seemed to settle on her shoulders as Jacquelyn escaped to her house. A.J.'s words from earlier pricked at her again like nettles: *huh, ice princess?*

Cold on the surface, cold within. Everybody, it seemed, sensed a basic lack in Jacquelyn—something missing down deep inside her. Some empathetic quality necessary to complete her femininity. But the empathy was there, all right, and anyone who sensed the chink in her armor pounded away at it incessantly, so the scab never got a chance to heal.

Ice princess…daughter of the ice queen. "I'll bet you even pee icicles," Joe had insulted her on the night he unceremoniously dumped her for Gina.

Suddenly huge tears welled in her eyes, and she sat on the edge of her couch. Mother was back in the big house, hiding in the basement, waiting for sundown and the night's first dose of anesthetic. Father was in his den, either arranging a bribe or a nooner. Yes…home sweet home!

Just why *should* she, Jacquelyn wondered, be able to nurture any belief in love? Who, in this travesty of a family, *could* have any confidence that they were worthy of love and affection—much less able to express it to others?

The phone on the table chirred. She cleared her throat, took a few deep breaths and picked it up.

"Hello?"

"*Y'all* requested one day's notice," A. J. Clayburn's mocking voice informed her without preamble. "So that's what *y'all* are getting. Be ready at sunrise tomorrow. I'll pick you up at your place."

"That's not a full day's notice. That's impossible. I—"

But she was protesting for the benefit of her own walls— the line went dead when he hung up on her.

Four

Jacquelyn had never bragged about being a morning person. Yet here she was, shivering in the damp chill well before sunrise, miserable as a draftee in the rain.

"C'mon, Boots," she urged her reluctant sorrel mare. "It's only the headstall, I promise. No cold bit in your mouth this time, honest, girl."

Boots, however, kept trying to back into her stall. She wanted nothing to do with any equipment this early in the morning. The seventeen-hand thoroughbred was well trained and of a sweet disposition. But Jacquelyn once made the thoughtless mistake, early on a cool morning like today, of slipping an unwarmed bit into the mare's mouth. Now Boots always rebelled at being rigged in predawn chill.

Jacquelyn shook the oat bag, gradually luring Boots back out of her stall.

"I know, girl, I know. This 'reliving Western history' is for the birds, huh? That's a girl, c'mon, that's a sweet lady."

Each time Boots exhaled, the breath formed a ghostly

wraith of smoke. This late in summer, Montana mornings had quite a snap to them. And Jacquelyn knew it would be even colder up in the high altitudes of Eagle Pass. As a native Georgian, she shared the Southerners' deep aversion to cold weather. Better a hurricane than a frigid night.

Last night she had crammed some warm clothing into a duffel bag along with her microrecorder and a notepad. But she still had to assemble all her riding gear. This rushing at the last minute was totally idiotic. She liked to plan carefully for a trip, with plenty of notice. Instead, she was being instantly ''mobilized,'' with Hazel and A. J. Clayburn her tyrannical, heartless commanders.

'''Atta girl,'' she praised when Boots, finally realizing she would not have to take the bit, dipped her head and let Jacquelyn slip a headstall on her. She tied a lead line to the ring and led her mare out into the grainy semidarkness of the corral.

She was carrying her saddle and pad out of the tack room when A.J.'s battered pickup rounded a rear corner of the house and parked in front of the corral gate. A two-stall horse trailer was hitched to the rear.

He somehow managed to poke his head out of the open window without disturbing his neatly crimped Stetson. He thumbed the hat off his forehead, grinning at her. The glare of a big sodium-vapor yard light cleanly illuminated the scornful twist of his mouth.

''Stir your stumps, girl!'' he called out the window. ''Time is nipping at our fannies. Drop that sissy saddle and let's hit the trail.''

''Hit the…? May I suggest we at least load up my horse and saddle?''

''Won't need 'em,'' he informed her curtly, turning off the engine and swinging down lithely from the truck.

Begrudgingly she felt a twinge of animal attraction to his good looks. But she shoved the feeling away as soon as she recognized what it was. Lust was sure not going to help her in the situation she was about to get herself into. It would only cause problems.

"Oh? I suppose I'll be riding double with you?"

A.J. glanced toward Boots. "As rare a privilege as that would surely be for me," he drawled with evident sarcasm, "it won't be necessary. Is that your horse?"

She nodded, staring up at him. He was still tall, even outside, with the mountains behind him tipped with the first pink buds of dawn light. Beside him she seemed inconsequential, and hopelessly female. No match at all.

He went back to the horse trailer and swung open the double doors.

"It's a good-looking animal," he conceded. "Good breeding and solid lines. That sorrel of yours is a fine flatland horse. Long-legged animals do real well in deep snow in open country. But we're going up into the mountains. That means we need good mountain ponies."

While he said this, he showed her the two horses in the trailer. That is, Jacquelyn *assumed* the two ugly, stubby-legged beasts were horses.

Despite her foul mood, she laughed so hard she almost dropped her saddle.

"Don't tell me," she managed between sputters of mirth. "You rescued them from a rendering plant?"

"Girl, you don't know nothing about horses, do you? These ain't riding-academy nags, they're genuine mountain mustangs. Some call 'em Indian scrubs. They've got the endurance of doorknobs."

She looked askance at their dish faces, bushy tails, and mongrelized confusion of colors and markings—no controlled bloodlines here.

"I won't ride a pretty horse like yours up in the mountains," he assured her, guessing her thoughts. "A pretty horse is a petted horse. And a petted horse is a spoiled horse."

Something aggressive in his tone hinted he wasn't talking just about horses.

She looked at him. By his glance he was obviously summing her up, taking in her designer black quilted barn jacket, her English custom-made paddock boots, and subtracting them from the value of her character. But then his gaze seemed to linger along the generous swells of her chest, and suddenly her net worth seemed to rise again.

It was still dark enough outside to hide the embarrassment heating her cheeks. Leave it to a macho redneck to view a woman like a piece of meat. But she supposed being a flank steak was better than an icicle.

She turned her attention back to the ponies. "Look, they're not just ugly. They're also so…little," she objected.

"'Praise the tall, but ride the small.' Sure, they're barely fourteen hands. But look at those short, thick, strong legs. That's what you need on rocky, narrow trails. These animals were born in the mountains, they're surefooted as wild goats. That bluegrass beauty of yours ever been up high in the rimrock in a forty-mile-an-hour wind?"

That goading twist to his mouth made her anger flare. She felt half-tempted to slap it right off his arrogantly handsome face.

"No," she admitted, resenting him for his know-it-all smugness and the way his eyes still seemed to lower to places below her neckline.

"You can leave that English saddle behind, too. I brought you a better one."

"*Better* one?" She snorted derisively. "I'll have you know this was custom-made for me at—"

"Sure, it's just fine—for a dog-and-pony show in London. But it'll be useless to you up in the mountains. Price tags ain't the issue. Up there you'll need something between your legs."

She flushed to the roots of her hair. "I beg your pardon?"

she demanded. Each syllable was so distinct it seemed chiseled.

He grinned. She was convinced he had see-in-the-dark eyes like a cat because she swore this time he saw her blush.

"Ease off, girl. I'm talking about a saddle horn. You'll need one to stay mounted on steep slopes."

He closed the trailer door on the mustangs.

"C'mon, girl," she called to her mare. "We'll let the cowboy have his eight seconds. You get to stay home."

She tried to coax Boots to come to her so she could lead the mare back into her stable. But the sorrel was excited by the presence of unfamiliar horses; she kept sidestepping away each time Jacquelyn tried to grab the lead line.

A.J. moved up beside her and gave a soft, fluting whistle. Boots answered with a friendly whicker, then trotted right over and nuzzled the hollow of his shoulder as if they were old and dear friends.

You damned traitor, she thought, watching her horse with a petulant frown. She grabbed the lead line and took Boots back toward her stall.

A.J. greeted her when she came back outside. "Hazel asked me to give you this." He added, smirking, "Seeing's how you took off so suddenly yesterday."

He slid a folded sheet of paper from the pocket of his vest.

"What is it?"

"An itinerary, I think she called it. Hazel's got some definite ideas how she wants this trip to be."

She started to unfold the sheet, but he stayed her hand with an iron grip. The calluses, thick on his palm, brushed her skin like friction burns.

"You can look at it in the truck," he told her brusquely. "I don't waste time when I've got something to do. Let's go."

She pulled her hand free. It tingled afterward, so much so she tucked it along with the sheet in the hip pocket of her jeans.

He had his door halfway open when she said, "Before we get going here, I just want to make one thing clear—while you seem to be very good at giving orders, I expect you to be my guide, not a drill sergeant. I'm going with you because my job has led me here. But it's not the rodeo ring, and I'm not one of your adoring fans you can tell jump."

"Not yet," he conceded with a whisper and an infuriating grin.

She took a deep breath to fire another salvo, but he stopped her by raising one hand like a traffic cop.

"Look, Scarlett, I ain't doing this baby-sitting job because I like your company, either. I'm doing a favor for Hazel. She put me in charge of this little excursion because I know where to go and how to get there. So let's get this straight from the start—when you're under my watch, I say how it's going to be, and that's the way of it. You don't like those terms, stay home. I'll tell Hazel you went puny on her."

Jacquelyn felt as if a steamroller had just gone over her. "You don't negotiate at all, do you?"

Again he trapped her in the full force of his metallic-gray gaze. "Depends what I'm after."

Her heart skipped.

He gave a harsh bark of scorn. "Now get in," he ordered, "or stay here. I'm damned if *I* care what a rich, spoiled, snot-nosed bawler like you does, but if you're not going, tell me so I can get these ponies back to their pasture before they founder."

She stared at him for a long moment. Then, for reasons she couldn't shape into words, she lumbered up into the passenger seat of the pickup.

They turned onto the road in strained silence, away from Mystery Valley to the eastern slopes of the Rockies.

As for the "itinerary" Hazel had sent along… Jacquelyn realized, only moments after unfolding the hand-drawn map, that the scheming cattle baroness had some grand design in mind.

She couldn't believe how detailed Hazel's notes were regarding what she was to write about. Not only was she to follow Jake's exact path, but Hazel insisted she was to camp in the same spots. The culmination of the trip was to be a night spent in the log cabin on Bridger's Summit—the original dwelling where Jake had taken his new bride on their honeymoon.

Numbly she folded the paper up and tucked it into her jacket. At least it's not the dead of winter, she consoled herself, staring at the man hunkered down in the seat next to her.

Still, she couldn't help thinking this trip was going to be a lot more grueling—and perhaps even dangerous—than it looked on paper.

The two-and-a-half-hour drive led them gradually lower, along tortuously winding mountain roads. Their route, according to Jacquelyn's map, roughly paralleled hidden Eagle Pass and McCallum's Trace.

The adventure still wasn't real to her. She looked at the man sitting next to her and wondered what kind of character he would ultimately prove to be. She would certainly know more about him on their return trip to Mystery.

He glanced at her and caught her staring.

She looked away, uncomfortable with the feeling of being virtually trapped with a man so utterly different from her that she lacked any vocabulary to describe him. A. J. Clayburn was indeed entirely unlike anyone she'd ever met before—and yet she couldn't deny a certain…fascination in watching the solid thigh and calf muscles bunch under his blue jeans as he worked the clutch and brakes.

The shared silence wasn't free of conflict. She had nothing against country-and-western music, in moderation. But she was convinced he deliberately kept the radio volume near full blast to unsettle her. And it was working. Her nerves jangled to every twang.

A little over an hour into their drive the road dipped

sharply, and the old pickup bounced hard like a tank leaping a ditch. One of the chrome radio knobs fell off.

She retrieved it from the floor, her head bumping into that same muscle-bunched thigh she had just been looking at. Flustered, she straightened and stuck the nob on the volume control.

"Perhaps with the money you make from guiding this trip," she suggested in a baiting tone, "you can put a down payment on a new pickup."

His sun-slitted eyes cut to her, then back to the road. The hat kept half of his face in shadow.

"If pickup trucks're status," he assured her, "then I got plenty. I drive this old gal because I happen to like her. The older the violin, the sweeter the music."

"Just a suggestion." She settled back against the worn seat. "I just figured a big rodeo star like you're supposed to be would want to show off a bit, that's all."

He gave a snort. "Stars live in Hollywood. And rodeo ain't my business, it's my love."

She waited, but he didn't volunteer any more information.

"Whatever your business," she offered, "Hazel certainly does speak well of you." Her tone also seemed to add *There's no accounting for taste.*

"Hazel and me think a lot alike. Especially about Mystery."

The accusation in his tone made her bristle. For a moment she pretended to stare at a dead snake she spotted hanging from a farmer's fence—a local custom to entice the rain. But his not-so-subtle reminder that she was an unwelcome outsider finally prompted her to retort.

"If you're trying to make some point about foreigners," she told him archly, "don't let *me* scare you."

"The *point* is simple. The empty spaces are dwindling out West. And stupidity and greed and Eastern capital will ruin them. Hazel is doing her best to fight it. But she might as well try to hold the ocean back with a broom."

"Because of people like me, you mean?"

"Maybe not you, exactly," he conceded reluctantly.

"But like my father, right? Trying to push through his Mountain View residential park with its aerial tramway?"

"Look, I was raised not to speak bad of a person's parents to their face. So I'll leave names out of it, okay? But we've got us a few folks around Mystery Valley that don't like boomtowners. We don't need people who come into town just to profit quick and then move on—leaving us with the mess."

She started to speak. But he pointedly reached over and cranked the radio volume back up, letting music drown her out.

"'Why is the rich man always dancing,'" he twanged along with the singer on the radio, "'while the poor man pays the band?'"

Around noon on Tuesday Hazel stepped outside into the coppery sunshine of her front yard. Her Prussian-blue eyes gazed toward the distant, serrated peaks of the mountains. If all had gone well this morning, by now A.J. and Jacquelyn should be on the trail.

"As the twig is bent," Hazel said softly to the beautiful summer day, "so the tree shall grow."

She'd done her level best to get her ambitious plan off to a strong start. If she did the thing right, then her beloved town would still be here generations from now—and still worthy of the love she felt for it. It was the perfect time to execute the plan. She was still sharp and plenty spry. And although she was still Montana's cattle queen, she had a topnotch foreman running most of the operation now. She had plenty of time for the one place on God's green earth she loved best of all. Her Mystery was more than just old buildings and monuments. It was also a collective legacy, the communal memory of a shared past. And perhaps most important of all: it was the home of ghosts who still lived there, their voices whispering in the skitter of autumn leaves, howling in the fierce winter winds.

Behind the old woman, in the kitchen, a radio deejay's voice droned on unnoticed.

"...this weather advisory just received here at KTIX in Lewistown. You cattlemen out there with stock up in the high-altitude summer pastures might want to drive them down to lower slopes during the next couple of days. The National Weather Service has just forecast a late-summer snowstorm for the front ranges of the northern Rockies. Up to thirty inches could be dumped on the peaks, greatly increasing the danger of avalanches and flash floods. Batten down, folks! Looks like *La Niña* can throw tantrums even in the Big Sky Country..."

Five

"**Y**ou'll ride this one," A.J. informed Jacquelyn in a curt tone that bordered on surly.

He led one of the geldings down the short ramp behind the trailer.

"It's a good animal, but tricky as a redheaded woman. Watch him, especially when you cinch the girth. He likes to hold in air so he can dump the rider later."

She studied the unlikely steed. The mustangs, with their stunted stature and barrel chests, struck her as ugly, ungracious animals. But they *did* have impressive muscle definition and powerful haunches.

"Yours is called Roman Nose," he added. "He was named after a renegade chief who led the Cheyenne Dog Soldiers in this area."

"I know who he was," she answered, impressed with his knowledge but unwilling to show it.

"Oh, yeah, that's right. *Y'all* do research, don'cha?"

By now she was too dismayed to rise to his bait. The

mountain ride wasn't the most brilliant endeavor she'd ever agreed to, but she was stuck with it now.

Or was she? She glanced all around, trying to decide if she was really going to do this.

The spot hardly seemed like an auspicious start to a ride Hazel promised would change her life. A.J. had referred to this area as a "jumping off place"—a little foothills hamlet called Truth or Dare, population 740. Last century it had been a stage-relay station. Now it was the last cluster of gas stations, restaurants and motels before the short-grass foothills gave way to the riotous upheaval of the Rocky Mountains.

"Heads up!" he shouted. He had moved to the bed of the truck and was tossing out supplies. Despite his warning, the pack he'd tossed toward her rolled into her legs hard enough to almost knock her down.

"Look," he told her, his face granite edged. "I ain't talking to hear my own voice. Pay attention! I said to start rigging your horse. You'll have to adjust those stirrups for your legs."

She sent him a resentful stare. Then she lugged the worn saddle over to where she'd tethered Roman Nose in a patch of lush grass. They were leaving A.J.'s truck and trailer parked safely in a lot behind a gas station on the western edge of town. From here the mountains were so close she could clearly make out the blue columbine and white Queen Anne's lace dotting their lower slopes.

Finding a spot to leave the truck and trailer had presented no problem for A. J. Clayburn. She had quickly learned he was a state-wide celebrity, not just a hero around Mystery Valley. They couldn't even finish a hasty meal at a local steakhouse without several fans recognizing him and requesting autographs. So much for his "stars live in Hollywood" baloney.

Roman Nose calmly chomped on grass while she spread the saddle blanket. Then, struggling with the unaccustomed weight, she tossed the saddle across the mustang's withers.

Unlike her English riding saddle, this one had a high pommel with a prominent horn and a high, narrow cantle to support the hips and back. A "working saddle" he had called it.

"Are you bolted to the ground?" His voice cut into her thoughts. "I'm rigged and ready to raise dust. C'mon, cottontail, get your head screwed on straight. I can't be wet-nursing you every foot of the way."

Hot anger flooded her. "In case you haven't noticed, I'm not some scuffed-boot cowboy you hired for a cattle drive. Go to hell."

"Nice kitty, rough tongue," he taunted before grabbing her arm and tossing her to the saddle like a sack of grain. She swore he even ran his hand down her rump in the scuffle. Certainly *that* hadn't been necessary.

"I mean it. I don't even want to be here. I'm doing this for Hazel," she spat.

"Same here. She's the *only* reason. Otherwise I'd avoid you like a smallpox blanket."

"Even for Hazel, I still have half a mind to call this off right now," she shouted at his retreating back.

"Fine by me. We ain't joined at the hip," he informed her indifferently as he secured a bedroll to his cantle with rawhide thongs. "Do what you want. Hazel expects you to show yellow, and so do I. Anybody can *write* about being tough."

She nibbled her bottom lip, torn with indecision. He deliberately ignored her, busy now securing a heavy sack of grain to his saddle horn. She had one strapped on, too. Since the horses would be working hard at a high altitude, they would need plenty of oats and corn for strength.

Hazel expects you to show yellow, and so do I.

"I'm almost ready," she mentioned as she bent to finish shortening the stirrups. She was almost finished when he dismounted and strode over to her, his stare filled with disapproval.

"What is it now?" she asked wearily. "My flannel shirt

isn't the proper pioneer color? My jeans don't have enough rivets in the pockets?''

"You got anything besides them show boots?" he demanded, meaning her low-heeled jodhpur boots of sleek oxblood calfskin. His hand rode on her calf. In her opinion, more unnecessary manhandling.

"These were hand-sewn in Dorset, England. They're worn by some of the world's top jockeys."

"That right, m'heart?" He squeezed her leg. His big hand seemed to circumvent her slender calf, enveloping it in warm steel. "Well, Eagle Pass ain't the Kentucky Derby. You ever try to keep flat heels in the stirrups on a rough ride?"

"I've been trained to avoid 'rough' rides," she informed him with icy hauteur.

He gave that one a hoot. "Well you're about to violate your training then. Good luck holding your stirrups with them buggy slippers."

"I'll manage," she assured him with confidence. "It's been many years since I've been thrown by a horse."

He sauntered back to his mount, lean-hipped and rangy, confident even in profile. His face was smug with the sly expectation of trouble ahead. At that moment she knew she truly hated the man.

"There's an old wrangler's rhyme," he told her. "'There ain't no horse that can't be rode, there ain't no man that can't be throwed.'"

"My God, Mr. Clayburn, you are so *quaint.* I'm duly impressed at your colorful Westernisms. Now if you'll just—"

She fell silent, her eyes widening when she spotted the blued metal of the rifle barrel. She watched him slide it from a buckskin sheath and transfer the weapon into a leather scabbard dangling from the fender of his saddle.

"What's that for?" she asked.

"Why, what else? In case you attack and try to ravish me. I hear you Southern gals have short fuses."

She didn't ask if he was alluding to tempers or passions. Nor did she want to know.

"I'll try so very hard to control myself," she said dryly. "Seriously, what's it for?"

"Bears and such," he replied, with what she was sure was a sly smile.

"Grizzly bears?"

"Not likely. But there's some good-size black bears. They take to the high country in summer."

"Are you…allowed to shoot them?"

"Not when they're mauling newspaper reporters. Look, if seeing a rifle gets you all nerve-frazzled, you're in for some shocks. Bears are only one danger up there. We've got high-water fords to cross, plus talus slopes so slippery even goats fall to their death sometimes. Lower down we'll have to watch for flash floods. And then—"

She wasn't sure of it, but she sensed a brief hesitation here—a momentary glitch in the veneer of his cool, confident authority before he went on.

"And then there's avalanches up higher."

"Avalanches? But…I mean, will we be riding through snow?"

His hand hooded his gaze. "We shouldn't have to. It'll be just above us at our highest point in the pass. But big sheets of old winter pack can slide off the outcroppings and shelves, and can fall on…anybody that's below," he finished with a grim face, reining his mount around. Both horses stood prancing, impatient at the delay.

"Now I'm sick of all your damn questions," he informed her. "We ain't gonna *talk* our way through Eagle Pass. Now, either we go or I'll drive you back to Mystery."

Biting her tongue, she followed, wondering what had set the man off. Only one thing was clear: she was going to spend five long days with him in the middle of nowhere. She was sure going to have the chance to find all his fuses.

* * *

Well, ain't *she* the big explorer, A.J. thought scornfully, slewing around in his saddle to watch Jacquelyn.

They were about two hours into their ride. She had halted Roman Nose beside the rotting timbers of an old head frame to dictate into her pocket recorder.

"I'm now passing the old Fitzsimmons-Phelps mine. Hazel told me it didn't exist yet when Jake McCallum rode past here. The first gold ore they pulled out was so high grade you could see the veins of gold in it. So much ore, in fact, that the wagons hauling it required up to twenty mule teams. Teams so long the drivers had to ride the lead mule. One freighter claimed a man could get rich just by following the ore wagons and picking up the shake."

Man alive, she *has* studied up plenty about those old times, he was forced to concede with grudging admiration. Nonetheless, the whole damn trip was nothing to him but one big cat-and-mouse game.

He had long despised the Rousseaux family and their summer-lodging, carpetbagging ilk. They had their permanent roots in Atlanta, yet felt they could lord it over everybody out in Montana. First the old man bought up the *Mystery Gazette,* and now he was trying to turn Mystery into a tract-house tourist mecca. And this high-toned daughter of his—wasn't *she* all silky satin?

A stir in his loins suddenly ticked him off even more. He sure as hell didn't want to play stallion to that Thoroughbred, no matter how beautiful she was. Hell, beautiful women were as easy to get for a rodeo man as a whore's token in Deadwood. He'd had his share and then some. Sure he never kept them, but he wasn't in it for the attachment.

No, beautiful women were around in heap and mounds. Women to love were actually pretty damn rare and something he wanted no part of. You loved; you lost. When he'd lost his parents in the blink of an eye, he never wanted to go through that agonizing gauntlet again. And the beautiful women, always around, made it real easy.

Gazing from the edge of his hat brim, he studied her. She was tiny but curvy. Just the way he liked a woman. The short-cropped hair revealed a fairylike delicacy to her face, but her soft, sensual, pink mouth and those damned sea-green eyes held no innocence. The mouth sometimes tightened in defense; the eyes filled with disapproval; but always a promise lingered in both, one that could pull a man toward her just by the darkness inside him.

She looked at him. The twist of her mouth proved she'd caught him staring this time.

But she ignored him and continued her essay.

Resenting her anew, he told himself she wouldn't be swaggering around a few days from now. The delicate magnolia would lose a petal or two. He'd guarantee it.

"I'm also looking," she narrated into her recorder, "at large patches of eroded slopes. Still denuded of timber, they are a legacy of that era. Some of the big mines had miles of tunnels. They had to be timbered against cave-ins. A few men got rich while the rest lived with the damage."

A.J. removed his hat to whack at flies with it.

"Hey, Ms. Ace Reporter!" he called back to her. "Them 'denuded' trees will grow back by the time you finish yakking to yourself! Let's make tracks. Now!"

She sent him the same go-straight-to-hell-and-do-not-pass-go glower that he'd seen from almost the beginning of the trip. Unfazed, he chuckled as he kicked his horse into motion again.

She's uppity now, he gloated. But she's headed for a fall. And not just because her saddle girth, despite my clear warning, is way too loose.

In spite of her gloomy mind-set, Jacquelyn soon reveled in the glorious beauty of the day.

The trail they followed through the rolling foothills was now so seldom used that it had grown over with grass and ground cover. Yet, never bothering with a compass or map, A.J. used familiar landmarks to orient them.

She'd been a fool to fear this experience, she assured herself. The clear air was cool and bracing against her skin. And the magnificent mountains, looming just ahead of them now, bristled with conifers on their lower slopes.

They reached a small, dry chasm and crossed it on a stone footbridge. Soon they reached a quiet pool fed by a runoff brook.

A.J. reined in ahead of her and swung down from the saddle.

"We best water the horses and fill our canteens," he told her. "This is the last low-country water hole."

Jacquelyn, too, dismounted and dropped Roman Nose's bridle so he could drink. She had to shade her eyes from the brilliant, late-afternoon sun.

Her good mood lulled her into a slightly less defensive frame of mind. Now she felt the strong presence of that other, more complete self trapped within her—the self who she knew was there, desperate to break through the thick layers of protective ice.

Watching him walk closer to the water, she again noticed the slight favoring of his injured leg. She recalled Hazel's description of his rodeo mishap, and a twinge of sympathy moved through her. While no rodeo devotee herself, she knew what rodeo was. She knew that saddle-bronc riding could be literally bone crushing. Just last month, up at the rodeo in Calgary, a contestant finished his ride and fell dead from the saddle.

"Hazel told me," she called over to him, overcoming her natural reticence, "that your last injury was pretty bad. That it may even threaten your rodeo career."

He turned away from the pool, twisting on the cap of a canteen. She saw a shadow move into his face.

"Hazel's top-shelf," he replied brusquely. "But she's a woman, so sometimes her tongue swings way too loose."

"Look, I didn't mean to touch any nerves."

"I guess where you come from, prying into other people's personal lives is just conversation. But out here we call it being nosy."

So much, she rebuked herself, for letting the ice thaw.

In the silence he nodded to her, once again all business. "There ain't no more bridges up ahead. I'd advise you to reset your saddle and check that girth again."

"I just checked it last time we stopped," she told him. "Why don't you worry about your own horse and let me tend to mine?"

He swung up and over, then reined his mustang around. He leaned forward and rested his muscular forearms on the saddle horn, watching her with that scornful twist to his handsome mouth.

"Yes'm, whatever y'all say," he told her in an exaggerated parody of her accent. "From now on, I'll just hush my li'l ol' redneck mouth."

Six

As a westering sun inched steadily toward the horizon, the two riders gradually left the foothills behind. Almost imperceptibly, they gained the front slopes of the mountains.

The going remained easy, at first. Mostly lush meadows dotted with wildflowers. And grass so tall that sometimes it literally polished their boots riding through it.

Jacquelyn's mood remained ebullient despite her guide's obvious hostility and surliness. The cool, sun-luscious air and grand, unending vistas more than compensated for the presence of the rigid, unyielding back of the cowboy she was forced to follow.

I couldn't warm up to him, she assured herself, if we were cremated together.

However, one problem had begun niggling at her: night was coming on. She knew where they would camp, of course, because it was marked on the map and the itinerary Hazel sent along—the same spot where Jake McCallum camped last century.

But she was beginning to wonder what their sleeping arrangements would be like. Suddenly feeling vulnerable so far from civilization, she wished she had gotten the plan clear while they'd been still in her own driveway. With the sun falling on the trail, now seemed no time to ask.

In the gear, she had noticed two down-stuffed sleeping bags and a small pup tent among the stuff A.J. had tossed out of the truck. But only one tent. Did he intend that small tent for *both* of them, she wondered. If so, she'd be sleeping in the open.

"Spell the horses," he called out, reining in ahead of her.

"Does everything have to be an order?" she asked. "We're not soldiers on bivouac."

He ignored her. He swung his leg over the cantle and dismounted, landing light as a cat. He began to unsaddle his horse.

"What...what are you doing?" she asked, angry at herself for stammering and revealing her sudden nervousness. "This isn't the first campsite. I thought this was just a rest stop."

"Sun's still hot," he replied curtly, tossing his saddle. "And so are the rocks. The saddle blankets are soaked with sweat. We don't dry them out now, tomorrow we'll have to put 'em on the horses wet."

He stared at her with those intruding, intriguing eyes.

"Start thinking more about the horses and less about your damn fingernails," he told her with blunt contempt.

"My grooming habits are none of your concern," she retorted.

"But my horses are," he shot out, "so pull that wet blanket off."

Biting her tongue, she swung down, untied the girth and tugged the heavy saddle off. The cowboy was right—damn his eyes, she thought. Despite the cool breeze and low humidity, the horses had been steadily climbing. The blanket *was* soaking wet.

She copied him, spreading it out on some sun-heated boulders beside the trail. While the blankets baked dry, they curried the dried sweat from the ponies.

A.J. remained taciturn, his face buried in the shadow of his hat. She saw him stare at something farther above them on the slope. A group of pronghorn antelopes—perhaps six or seven—were picking their way down from the granite peaks high above, shrouded in clouds.

"Hmm," he said, as if to himself. "That's odd."

"What is?"

"Pronghorns generally forage by themselves. You'll rarely see a group moving as one like that."

"Hunters?" she suggested.

"Nah, not up there—no access road. Might be some weather heading up."

He didn't sound worried about it. So she wouldn't worry, not with the day so clear and glorious. It made bad weather seem as remote as a distant rumor of war.

But the day *was* waning, she reminded herself. Soon the awkward moment would arrive when they'd have to clarify certain matters—better to cool this noble savage's blood now than later, when it might be more difficult.

The last thought sent a little flutter of nervousness through her stomach. Sure, Hazel vouched for the guy. But what did Hazel know about his sexual manners? The day wasn't even over and he'd already eyed her enough to assess her bra cup size and had manhandled her with the thoroughness of a physician. If he thought he was going to bunk with her, too, he was dead wrong.

Jacquelyn cast about for some diplomatic way to broach the subject. But she finally simply blurted out, "What about…sleeping arrangements?"

His eyes flicked to hers, sly and knowing, and she blushed like a schoolgirl.

"No problem," he assured her. "I figured we'd just sleep in a Tucson bed."

"I…what's that?"

"Y' lie on your stomach and cover herself with your back," he said from a deadpan.

She stared at him, not quite getting it.

He laughed.

"Seriously," she said. "What—"

"You worry too much, Miss Rousseaux," he tossed out.

"I'm a woman. I've a right to know sleeping arrangements."

"Look, it's damn easy for us men to control our carnal urges when there's nothing special to *urge* us. There's plenty of fillies in my stable, if you take my meaning. Don't worry about me peeking at your cute little bare butt. I ain't woman starved."

"Why you arrogant, self-centered—"

"Blankets are dry enough," he grunted, cutting her off. "Saddle up and spare me your guff."

Fuming at her companion, she still did as ordered. But preoccupied by her anger, she failed to check the girth twice.

"Not too far from this big erosion gully," Jacquelyn narrated into her pocket recorder, "is the spot where Jake's horse stepped into a gopher hole. When the determined young pioneer broke his left arm in the fall, he set it himself with a canteen strap."

The sun still showed, but only as a dull orange ball balanced on the western horizon. According to Hazel's map, they would soon cross Crying Horse Creek. Then they would make their first camp.

The air was beautiful in the dying light, spun-gold gauze, softening all it touched like a flattering airbrush. Again, as she retraced Jake's actual steps, the enchantment of the story assignment transported her, like listening to mystic chords.

"The love that Jake and Libbie McCallum felt for each other," she spoke ardently to her recorder, "was matched by their love of this rugged but beautiful new country. One love melded into another, forming a complete, uninterrupted circle. It was, in one very real sense, a love as big and grand and endless as the American West itself.''

She turned off the recorder and slipped it into a saddle bag. While she did so, she noticed A.J. suddenly pivoting around in his saddle. He gave her a long hard look, then resumed the trail.

''So what was that about?'' she nudged.

''I guess I'm beginning to see why Hazel let you come on this trip. You really know how to put one word after another.''

He actually seemed to be complimenting her. Cautiously she replied, ''I hope I can. That's my profession.''

''Yeah, like you need a profession when your old man's worth a mint.''

It was her turn to stare at him. Naturally, she told herself, the beast would have to ruin any good impulse he had.

She pressed her lips into a grim, straight line and did her best to ignore him.

Soon, however, another problem edged his surliness out of her thoughts. For some time now she had heard the increasing churn and roil of swiftly moving water. Abruptly, she rounded the shoulder of a big knoll, and her stomach went cold at the sight ahead.

''*That's* Crying Horse Creek?'' she lamented, straining to be heard above the noise. '''Creek?' My God, it's a river!''

''Most of the year it's just a creek,'' he assured her. ''But twice a year they open the catch-basin gates up at Point Cheyenne Reservoir. That water is snowmelt, so it's damned cold. Push through it quick.''

''Push through it?'' she repeated, dazed.

The clear water flowed so swiftly in the middle it was actually churning foam.

His horse was already heading down the grassy bank, showing little concern.

''Don't do a thing except to hang on,'' he called back over the rapid chuckle of the current. ''Just sit your saddle and keep the reins slack. These horses are strong swimmers. They'll do all the work.''

''I don't think—*oh!*''

Seeing his companion wade into the raging creek, Roman Nose surged quickly ahead, catching her by surprise.

She managed to take hold of the saddle horn and regain her balance. But even as Roman Nose plunged into the creek, snorting, the gelding gave a sinewy little twist that sent her sliding to the right—or rather, sent the loose saddle sliding and her with it.

She gasped in shock as she plunked unceremoniously into the frothing water, so cold she felt as if she was plunging naked into a snowbank.

Roman Nose simply swam on toward the opposite bank without her, whickering to announce his clever victory over his rider.

Jacquelyn was a good swimmer under reasonable conditions. But wearing boots and heavy jeans while fighting a swift current hardly constituted reasonable conditions.

At first, tumbled about like so much driftwood, she couldn't even orient herself to start swimming. Besides, there were good-size boulders in the water. She had to worry about protecting her head. It was all she could do to tread water while the current washed her rapidly downstream.

And it was *cold*…so cold so quickly, already she was numb and her back teeth were chattering hard.

''Rope!'' she heard A.J. shout. ''Grab the rope!''

What rope, she wanted to scream. *What* damned—?

It literally slapped her face. He had looped it in accurately.

She reached out, seized rough hemp and felt herself being tugged through the worst of the raging current.

Once out, she staggered up onto the bank, looking and feeling like a drowned rat. A.J. stood there above her, strong white teeth flashing as he laughed in unbridled glee.

'' 'It's been many years since a horse has thrown *me,*' '' he mimicked in his wretched imitation of her accent.

She was too cold to care about feeling humiliated. The day was cooling quickly as sunset approached, and now each spirited breeze cut into her wet flesh like a blade.

Her spare clothing would have remained dry in the waterproof pack. But she glanced around and felt her stomach sink—absolutely *no* cover for even minimal modesty.

He read her dilemma and sent her a goading little grin. "Guess you'll want to get out of them wet things, huh?"

"It can w-wait." She shivered. The campsite was only a half mile farther. There would be trees there to hide behind.

"Go ahead," he urged her, making a show of placing a hand over his eyes. "Peel 'em off. I won't peek. Cross my heart."

"N-no, thanks. Let's just g-go on."

Forcing herself to move, she reset her saddle and carefully cinched it. Wincing at the cold contact of wet clothing, she was about to hoist herself into the saddle when a warm, strong hand stopped her.

"Don't read too much into this, Miss Rousseaux, but I ain't bringing no corpse back to Hazel. Hypothermia is quick. Now get out of those wet clothes. And get out of them now."

She stared up at him, every muscle in her body shivering. "There's no privacy here for me to change."

"Ahh, well, it don't matter if you strip buck," he assured her, still staring at her with those cool, piercing eyes. "Wet like you are, I can already see plenty of what you got."

Mortified, she looked down at her wet shirt plastered across her chest. The pale pink broadcloth might as well have been the filmiest negligee in the lingerie store. And her glossy pink spandex bra now looked as transparent as cellophane. A professional stripper couldn't have devised a more titilating outfit.

Folding her arms across her breasts, she glared at him like a rabid cat. "I thought you j-just said you have n-no interest in looking at me," she spat.

"No," he corrected her. "I said I'm not woman starved. But there's nothing wrong with my appetite."

"Save it for your 'fillies,'" she fired back, shivering violently as she went to the other side of Roman Nose and fumbled for the dry clothes in her pack.

Now how was he going to get *that* out of his mind, A.J. asked himself as he refilled his canteen from Crying Horse Creek. This trip that he thought would be nothing more than putting an uppity woman in her place was proving to be much more complicated. Jacquelyn Rousseaux was not his type of woman at all, but every now and then she got this strange, wistful expression in those sea-colored eyes of hers, and he felt himself relenting, lowering his guard one more fraction. Now he was going to have to make camp, and all he was going to see in his mind's eye for the rest of the night was her, spitting mad, wet, cold and nearly naked from the waist up. He closed his eyes even now. The way she was built she sure looked good from the waist up.

Glancing behind him, he got a timeline of her changing her clothes. All he could see, with Roman Nose blocking the way, was her legs and the damp tousled top of her head. But then the wet pink blouse came off. He knew it because she dropped it at her feet. The bra followed, falling in a limp pile. Then she peeled off her saturated jeans, and he got a nice gander at trim shapely legs. But then a pair of pink panties to match the bra dropped to the pile. He had to adjust himself twice in the interim.

"Get a move on, girl," he barked, intentionally trying to rattle her.

For a long moment, she fiddled with something, then drew a fleece shirt over her head and stepped into her jeans.

"I'll be ready in a s-second," she stammered, her teeth still chattering. She came around to the other side of her pony and fiddled with the buckle of her saddle bag. She didn't seem to notice but the bra dangled from the pile in her arms and fell to the ground, still unseen.

He straightened and went over to her. Picking up the bra, he ran his thumb pensively over the underwire. He'd seen a hundred of the things in his time, but this one seemed different somehow. More fragile, more seductive, more dangerous.

"Thank you," she said stonily as she grabbed it out of his hands.

His eyes locked with hers.

An unwelcome acknowledgment sizzled between them.

She stuffed the bra into her saddle pack. "I'm ready. Let's go," she rasped.

"Gotta make up some time," he ordered before slinging himself into the saddle.

It was suddenly all business again, but something had changed between them. And all he could think about from that moment forward was wet, translucent pink fabric and eyes he wanted to make dark with pleasure.

Seven

The first camp Jake McCallum made while crossing the Rocky Mountains was in a pine-sheltered hollow on the middle slopes. By the time A.J. and Jacquelyn reached the spot, it was bathed in the last fading sunlight.

Though Jacquelyn had changed into dry clothes, she was still so thoroughly chilled she couldn't keep from trembling. With shaking fingers she untacked her pony and brushed him down. Then when A.J. was busy using a hatchet to strip kindling bark from an old log, she retrieved her wet clothes from the saddle bag and draped them out of his view over a tree limb.

When he'd built a fire, she couldn't help but inch closer to it to relieve her incessant shivering. Seeing her, he held up a piece of nylon fishline with a hook attached. "I'll be taking care of your supper. So you take care of the horses' supper."

She went to work without a word, her thoughts disturbing and uncharitable.

While she occupied herself with the mustangs, he disappeared into the gathering darkness of the trees.

It took her a good bit of time to tend to both horses. She moved a little slower than usual, her back sore from hours against that narrow, high cantle, her fingers still frozen from her fall in the "creek." With the sun gone, the night chilled quickly. She was happy to finally settle on a warm rock near the fire when her task was finished.

The insect noise of the night rose steadily, like the hum of power lines. Blazing flames from the fire crackled and sent off little glowing streams of sparks. She breathed in the strong odor of pine resin.

But despite the peacefulness of the moment, the darkness around her was deep and foreboding. Even being dumped in a rustic camp in Montana couldn't alter the fact that she was an urban creature. The darkness seemed to lurk like a mugger in the shadows, waiting to pounce on her.

A stick snapped somewhere beyond the glow of the fire, and she tensed, straining to see in the gloom. But she had ruined her night vision by staring directly into the flames.

Another stick snapped, behind her this time.

She rose from the boulder she was seated on and turned to stare into the dark maw of the night.

"A.J.?" she called. "Is that you?"

The silence mocked her. A frog croaked, and somewhere nearby an owl hooted. The insect hum rose to a tense crackle.

Leaves rustled somewhere to her left. Her veins iced over.

"A.J.?" she called again, louder this time. "Is that—?"

A hand clasped her shoulder from behind, and she cried out in fright. She whirled around to face A.J.'s insulting grin. He held up two fat trout for her inspection.

"Little jumpy, ain't you?"

"That wasn't funny," she stated, backing away from his intrusion into her personal space.

"The hell it wasn't," he contradicted as he started cleaning the fish on a rock. "Matter fact, you're funnier than a rodeo clown. I'm starting to like this trip. Y'all," he added.

"There's…something out there," she said nervously, still staring beyond the fire. "I heard noises. Noises that weren't you."

"There's plenty out there," he agreed as he rubbed the juice from a few wild onions onto the trout. "Bears, snakes, coyotes, cats, skunks, raccoons, porcupines. Surprised your friends back east haven't figured out some way to charge them rent."

He cleared a little corner of the fire and laid the trout directly onto the glowing embers. He turned them often with his knife, basting them with more onion juice. They baked quickly. It was easy to peel the scorched outer layer away, exposing the tender and savory part.

The simple meal tasted delicious to Jacquelyn. Especially with the appetite she'd worked up. Already, even this ridiculously early, her muscles and eyelids were growing heavy. She was working up her courage to once again bring up the awkward topic of sleeping arrangements.

However, he preempted her. He crossed to the pile of gear. Then he returned to her side of the fire and tossed the folded-up tent and one sleeping bag onto the ground beside her.

"There's your private hotel room," he informed her. "No room service. And the bathroom is the second tree to your left. If you get scared during the night," he added, "tough toenails. Don't go bothering me. I need my beauty rest."

"Aren't you at least going to set up the tent?" she demanded as he swaggered away. "I've never done it before."

"Good time to earn your first merit badge, huh? Nobody waited on Jake, either."

"But *you're* the guide. Hazel hired you for my care."

"This ain't the Ritz, and I don't live in your damn pocket. Out West, a guide ain't a houseboy. He's a pathfinder, a scout. You're damn lucky I even fed you. When you can do for yourself, you're expected to."

"Eight seconds on the back of a bucking horse," she fumed, "and you think it makes you a tin god. You sure are smug for someone who uses the word *ain't* all the time."

"Listen, cottontail," he called over as he spread out a canvas groundsheet for his sleeping bag. "I know it's full of snobs back East where you come from. But out here there's always been only two social classes—the quality and the equality. And so far, you ain't neither."

"It's *either*," she ranted, wondering if all his taunting was making her lose her mind. "*Either.* 'You *aren't* either.'"

"Whatever you say. G'night, sugar britches."

Jacquelyn finally managed to get the small tent staked down, though one side caved in on her almost immediately. But she was too exhausted to worry about fixing it.

The day had begun well before sunrise. The drive, the ride, her plunge into frigid Crying Horse Creek—all that, plus the emotional roller coaster of being at the mercy of A. J. Clayburn had taken its toll. She fell asleep almost at once, as if drugged.

But though she slept deeply, peace of mind still eluded her.

She was not plagued with nightmares exactly. Just eerily unpleasant dreams with no apparent point except to make her hate herself. Long, agonizing dream sequences featuring Joe and Gina. Tender love scenes, intimate moments that radiated warmth and spontaneity, which she was always staring at from outside, behind a cold pane of glass, alone and destitute in the falling snow.

And she saw herself narrating into her pocket recorder. But it wasn't her voice coming from her. Instead, other voices threw accusations at her like narrators in some absurd Fellini film, voices that didn't go with the images.

Or did they?

Her mother's voice: *After all, baby, decorum should rule everything. Even a Southern debutante's failed life.*

Hazel's voice: *This world belongs to the living...I assure you, making this journey will change your life.*

The cowboy's voice: *What would you know about being turned on? Is that something you've "researched," too?*

From the first moment that Jacquelyn woke up, something felt wrong.

For one thing she lay on her back. She had never been able to sleep on her back.

An urgent inner voice warned her. She sensed the weight on her stomach. The foreign weight. Like a hand pressing down on the lower part of her stomach.

For a moment she was on the verge of using her left hand to check it out. But the urgent inner voice warned her to be still.

Still as stone.

Very slowly she lifted her head to take a better look around her. The fly of the tent had worked open a crack, perhaps when the one side collapsed. And evidently she must have gotten too warm during the night—her sleeping bag was closed but she'd left it unzipped to a point just above her navel.

Open tent, open bag...and something definitely sharing the bag with her. Something seeking warmth during the night.

Sweat broke out on her face, and she felt her heart surge on a spurt of adrenaline. She looked down into the darkness of her sleeping bag. Along with the fear came a powerful sense of revulsion.

She knew most snakes weren't poisonous. But Montana still had rattlesnakes. And though the bite from just one wasn't usually fatal for an adult, it could be—especially this far from any medical help.

She fought to gain control of her breathing. The weight had stirred against her, as if reacting to her fear responses. Thank God she'd slept fully clothed. Otherwise the snake would be rubbing its rough scales against her bare skin. That thought brought a wave of nausea that she barely fought down.

She could see gray, grainy light beyond the open fly of the tent. Just barely dawn.

She mustered her courage. "A.J.," she called out softly. Nothing. He *said* he slept like a baby, damn him.

"A.J.?" she called out again, a little louder this time. Again the weight stirred against her, intimate and disgusting.

"I don't serve breakfast in bed," his sleepy, irritated voice replied just when she'd given up hope he would hear her.

"A.J., my God, help me," she breathed out slowly. "There's a snake in my sleeping bag."

"Just lie real still," his voice answered immediately, wide awake now and closer to the tent. "It should be in a stupor from your body heat. They can be grabbed by the head if it's done quick."

Her neck got tired and she had to lower her head again. But she could hear the slithering whisper as he opened the fly of the tent wider. Then she saw him carefully maneuvering, shoehorning himself into the cramped space beside her sleeping bag.

"Easy does it," he whispered to her as his right hand eased into the bag. "Just lay there and don't move a hair."

He still carried the pleasant smell of the campfire with him. He was bare from the waist up, and even in this stingy light his muscles stood out like taut ropes.

She felt his hand move over the swell of her breasts. In the back of her mind, she seemed to think he paused there. Her anger was tempered only by her fear. "I don't believe you. Any cheap excuse to cop a feel."

"You want me to get the snake out of the landscape or protect your modesty? Choose or I leave."

He started to slide his hand back out.

She almost asphyxiated in her panic. "No! Please!" she pleaded. "I'm sorry. *Please* just get it off me, A.J."

"You women and your damn serpents," he muttered. "I better at least get an apple out of this."

He slid his hand in again, easing it cautiously lower. But the intrusion had disturbed the snake. She almost screamed when it moved even lower, as if retreating from his hand. She could feel it now, sheltered in the valley formed where her thighs joined.

"It went lower," she whispered, lips trembling with fear.

He nodded. "I saw the shape move. Now I know which end's the head." And he added, the grin returning, "Oh, to be that snake's head right now."

She wanted to slap him, but she didn't dare move. She felt his hard callused hand slide down the flat plane of her stomach. It moved even lower, and despite her rigid fear, her body reacted on its own to the intimate, if unavoidable, caress.

"Close?" he asked her, torturing her with obvious relish.

She almost wimpered. "Very."

"Gotcha!" he exclaimed, suddenly withdrawing his hand.

Mercifully, she got only a quick look at the approximately three-foot-long reptile as he pulled it out of the tent.

"Hell," he scoffed, turning it loose on the ground, "it's just a harmless gopher snake."

Shaking, she peeled the sleeping bag off and scrambled from the tent. By now there was enough light to clearly make out the camp.

He suddenly burst out laughing. "You Southern gals *are* fast, huh?"

"What's that supposed to mean?" she demanded.

"Hell, we've only spent one night together. And already you've let me run my hand down your pants. From my neck of the woods, that's third base, ain't it?"

"God, I hate you," she fumed, turning her back on him to disassemble the tent.

"Was it that good for you, too?" he taunted.

She could see his smile as if she had eyes on the back of her head.

Eight

With the terror of the snake incident behind her, Jacquelyn felt a deep embarrassment set in. Thanks to her own bumbling stupidity, she had placed herself once again—and this time *literally*—in the cowboy's hands. Twice already he had rescued her from herself.

And to make matters worse, she wondered if she had actually enjoyed his humiliating groping of her—certainly her traitorous body had. A.J., no doubt, had noticed the sudden change in her breathing, her passive acceptance of his more-intimate-than-necessary touch.

The same traitorous body, she realized as she took her first steps of the new day, was also hopelessly saddlesore. Now that her fear was gone, she became aware of the throbbing ache in her legs and lower back. Her tailbone felt like someone had been beating on it with a hammer.

But when he saw her limping, he only flashed that scornful twist of his mouth.

"I've figured something out." She flung the words at him

as she ran a brush through her sleep-tangled thatch of platinum hair.

"Go tell." He was using a stick to stir up the embers from last night's fire.

"Yes, I see it very clearly now. The more miserable I am, the better your mood seems to be."

He snorted.

"Hazel failed to mention the trial of being trapped in your company," she fired at him. "As much as I'd love to stay and bathe myself in the glow of your brilliant wit, I'd rather bath myself in a nearby stream. May I ask where you caught those trout last night?"

A.J., busy crumbling kindling bark onto the embers, rolled his head over his left shoulder. "Little pool back yonder about a hundred yards or so. Think you can manage to fall in?"

Blushing again at the thought of how she had looked yesterday in the wet pink blouse, she walked off without a word, carrying a towel with a jar of cleansing cream, her compact and a few other items rolled up inside it.

"Watch out for bears," he warned behind her. "There's some in the area—that's what you heard last night. I found tracks."

She had no way of knowing when this difficult man was being truthful with her. But she thought about those noises she'd heard, and a little electric tingle of fear moved up her spine. She refused, however, to give him the pleasure of showing more fear than he'd already been privy to.

The pool he'd indicated was fed by a bubbling runoff spring, so the crystal-clear water was ice-cold. But it was bracing on her skin as she splashed herself awake, shivering at the contact.

She made a rueful frown as she studied her face in the compact mirror. That beautiful skin Hazel had complimented her on was starting to wind chafe. She cleaned and patted dry her face. Then she brushed it lightly with blush, wondering if Hazel would disapprove of such "fripperies" on the trail.

She had turned to gaze at her rippling reflection in the water when leaves rustled nearby. Barely conquering the urge to bolt in panic, she hurried back to camp.

It was then she realized her growing dependence on A.J. And she damn well resented it.

She eyed him balefully while he rolled up his sleeping bag and ground sheet.

"We ain't got all morning while you paint your face," he told her in a churlish tone. "You want any breakfast, better eat it now and eat it fast. I'm saddling up in five minutes."

"Ja, mein herr!" she retorted with military precision. But then she realized from his comment that he must have been watching her at the stream, putting on her blush, and a small frisson passed through her.

Hazel's detailed instructions included a request to also re-create Jake McCallum's simple meals along the trail. While Jacquelyn was gone, A.J. had mixed cornmeal with water, then tossed the meal balls directly into the hot ashes to bake. Hot corn dodgers and unsweetened black coffee strong enough to "float horseshoes," as Jake had described his re-past, made a basic but adequate meal.

The sun was just barely over the eastern horizon by the time they resumed the upward trek. Once they'd cleared the trees, Jacquelyn turned to gaze behind them. Below, mattresses of fog still covered the valleys.

Her microrecorder had survived the spill into Crying Horse Creek. She started to describe the scene below them. However, A.J. gave her no time now to contemplate nature's beauty. He began, once again, to lecture her about the dangers ahead. It soon became clear to her that he was really trying to scare the daylights out of her.

"Sometime tomorrow," he informed her in ominous tones, "we're going to reach Devil's Slope."

"Yes, I saw it marked on Hazel's map. Is it steep?"

"Is Paris a city? But steep ain't the half of it. It's several hundred yards of trail littered with loose shale and volcanic scree. Straight cliffs on both sides. Even mountain goats have been known to slip and go over them cliffs. I'm serious—you might want to make out a will before we cross it. Maybe scrawl down some last sweet nothings for your boyfriend back in Georgia."

"I ain't got no boyfriend in Jaw-juh," she shot back, mimicking him mimicking her.

He seemed inexplicably pleased.

Rather than play further into his game, she abruptly changed the subject.

"How do you know Hazel, anyway? I mean, it's obvious you feel intensely loyal to her."

He took a long moment to answer her, as if he was deciding her worthiness of his rare—and then almost always acerbic—words.

Finally he said, "When the Clayburns came out here right after the Great Depression, they were so dirt poor their babies had to wear flour-sack diapers. But see, the McCallums never measure how deep a person's pockets are. They only care about the depth of their character. Hazel's daddy gave my grandpa a homestead. A whole quarter section."

"A quarter section?"

"A hundred and sixty acres. That's tiny, for a Western ranch. Not even a ranch, really. Graze being what it is out here, a typical spread might have forty thousand head roaming a few hundred thousand acres. But see, our section was river bottom and covered with timber. Right when the Burlington and Northern Railroad was desperate for ties. That money got us started."

Started toward what, she wondered. A rattletrap pickup truck? Some dynasty.

"Anyhow," he resumed, still eyeing the trail ahead, "it's a point of honor with my family never to refuse a request by a McCallum."

"I see. So when Hazel called, you were ready. Even though you'd rather pull your own jaw teeth out than spend time with a snotty rich bitch like me?"

He glanced around at her and flashed that sarcastic grin, his metallic eyes piercing her like a pair of bullets.

"The way you say," he confessed. "And some day my kids'll be doing the same. If not for Hazel herself, then for the town of Mystery. Because it's our home, a home she and her kin built alongside mine."

She lapsed into a pensive silence, mulling over all he'd told her. Despite her antipathy toward A.J., she envied him. Like Hazel, he had experienced a sense of permanence, a sense of belonging and place, in Mystery.

She contrasted that to her own "privileged" upbringing. But when you're rich, with a half dozen houses to the family name, you end up with no real home to speak of. Especially when neither of your parents ever felt obligated to provide any sense of family. Just unrelenting criticism from her father and alcohol-induced cynicism from her mother.

"Hazel," he summed up, "is one of those rare folks who can live her dream and get others to dream right alongside her."

For some reason she couldn't name, his words struck her with the force of physical blows. Rare, unexpected tears stung in her eyes. *Unlike you, Little Miss Freeze, she's got a warm and beating heart—not a chunk of cold stone.*

Blinking back the tears, she turned silent, and asked no more questions.

As the morning heated up, huge blow flies began to harass both horses and riders. But Jacquelyn noted that she and the cowboy had ascended high. Not only were the trees thinning, but she could spot beautiful gorges below them, white water frothing through.

A.J. seemed to be studying the sky a lot, his eyes slitted

in a vague frown. She couldn't see why—no dark clouds showed anywhere.

The slope had steepened, and they stopped more often to let the horses blow. Twice he called a halt to spread their sweaty saddle blankets in the sun, drying them.

He *is* careful of the horses, she thought. And though she would be damned if she'd admit it out loud, she approved. Unlike his views of her, A.J. seemed to see himself as the horse's partner, not its master. His respect surprised her, especially in light of his bronco riding, a profession known for dominating the horse's will.

"Right now," he called back to her late in the morning, "we're passing an old Indian meeting place called Council Rock. The Sioux and their Cheyenne cousins used to meet here and plan their battle strategy against the bluecoat invaders."

She studied the huge, table-shaped slab of metamorphic rock. It wasn't marked on Hazel's map.

"May we stop here for a few minutes?"

He nodded and swung down from the saddle. "Horses could use a break, anyway."

So could *I,* she fumed to herself. But then, I've only got two legs, so I don't count.

She dismounted and began searching the stony ground in this oval-shaped hollow. Within minutes she felt a surge of excitement when her toe unearthed an arrowhead of flaked flint.

"I got a cigar box full of them," he scoffed, bored when she showed it to him. "Plus one my great-great-granddaddy dug out of his own thigh back in Iowa."

"Well, we can't all be as world wise and grizzled as the great A. J. Clayburn," she pointed out. "*I'm* excited."

"That makes twice today," he returned, his shadowed gaze raking her.

She felt the blood flush her cheeks, unable to stop thinking about the sleeping-bag incident.

"You assume an awful lot," she quipped lightly. But she turned away from his mocking gaze, thumbing on her pocket recorder.

"I'm looking down on the low country from a spot along McCallum's Trace known as Council Rock. As I hold an arrow point in my hand, I am reminded of the Indian legend that says the spirit of Manitou rules all these mountains. Anyone who looks at them once, claims the legend, will always be called back."

Behind her, he made whooping sounds like a Hollywood redskin. He hoisted himself into the saddle again.

"Paleface girl named Snake in Pants make heap big noise," he shouted.

Heat surged into her face at his deep-chested laugh. She untied Roman Nose's hobbles and mounted, suddenly too angry to care about striking vistas or Indian history.

However, the steeping trail had reached a stretch littered with shale and loose talus. A.J. had jogged slightly to the right to avoid it. But Jacquelyn, still ruminating over her thoughts about her "guide," rode right into the unstable slope.

"Look out!" she heard him shout. "Wake the hell up, you little fool!"

But he was too late. Even as she realized her mistake, Roman Nose planted a foreleg on a piece of unstable shale. It gave way with a skittering scrape, and suddenly she and her horse were literally sliding backward.

With the instinct of a show rider, she started to tighten the reins.

"Don't try to control it!" he shouted. "Just grab your pommel and hold on!"

She followed orders. The sturdy little mountain horse had turned into a virtual sled. She wasn't sure how many yards they slid backward with Roman Nose fighting to stay on his feet, but the mustang finally won his battle with gravity—they came to a jolting stop with no harm done.

No harm, but she knew her face was still as pale as moon-stone when she reached A.J. above. He clearly relished the terror in her eyes.

"You best nerve up," he goaded her as they started upward again. "Devil's Slope ain't that far ahead. Only, you'll have cliffs to worry about, too."

"Well, if I do go over," she retorted tightly, "I'll have the consolation of being rid of you, won't I?"

"Actually," he corrected her, trying to suppress his grin, "since I'd be the one still alive, technically I'd be rid of *you.*"

Late on Wednesday afternoon, the second day of A.J. and Jacquelyn's journey through Eagle Pass, Hazel called the park ranger station at Cheyenne Mountain. Last night, check-ing the TV Weather Channel as ranchers habitually did, Ha-zel had learned of the severe blizzard approaching the high country.

"National Park Service, Cheyenne Mountain," a booming basso profundo voice answered.

"Bob, that you? This is Hazel McCallum calling from Mystery."

"Hazel, how you doing, young lady?" replied Bob Jo-hannson. "Kinda high jinks you up to now?"

"Bob, I've heard the storm warning. You got any weather up there yet?"

"Nah. But some signs it's coming. The high-country ani-mals are heading to lower ground. But if it's your summer pastures you're worried about, Hazel, don't fret your cattle. Won't be any snow or freeze below the tree line."

"Oh, my herds are fine, Bob. It's a young couple I'm a little worried about. A. J. Clayburn and my neighbor, Jac-quelyn Rousseaux. They just set out yesterday morning on a horseback trip from the foothills. They're heading up to the pass along McCallum's Trace."

There was a slight pause on Bob's end, and Hazel felt a

little quickening of apprehension. Even a good plan could go bad.

"Not the best place to be right now," Bob allowed. "That is, if this storm turns out like some're saying it might. Those two wouldn't happen to have a two-way radio or a cell phone with them?"

"No, and that's my stubborn fault. This trip is to commemorate Jake McCallum's ride for the sesquicentennial. Jacquelyn is a reporter for our local newspaper. I made a big stirring and to-do over how this trip had to be authentic and historical. Bob, I hope this time I wasn't too clever for my own good. I don't suppose you could send a man over their way? Maybe use your helicopter?"

"Hazel, for you? That chopper would be on its way now if I had it. But you know about the forest fires down in the Powder River Valley, right? The governor ordered our bird down there to drop fire retardant. Without a chopper, we'd never get up near the trace in time to warn them."

"No," Hazel agreed, "no way you could do it. But at least I tried."

"Buck up, Hazel. No bad weather yet. Maybe it'll blow over. Besides, if it's A. J. Clayburn with that gal, they should be all right. A.J. could follow you into a revolving door and come out ahead, he's that sharp."

Hazel laughed, seeing the truth of this. After she hung up, she went out into the side yard and gazed toward the distant mountain peaks. Bob was right, of course, about A.J. Common men did not win the World Cup in *any* rodeo event, most certainly not saddle-bronc riding. That same competence and tenacity gave those a strong survival edge.

But a high-country blizzard was its own kind of cruel master. Even Jake, all grit and a yard wide, admitted he only survived because no blizzards caught him in the mountains.

"Lord," Hazel said softly, "my intention was to save Mystery with some new blood settling in. I did not mean to place an inexperienced, scared little slip of a girl smack in the middle of a natural disaster.''

Then again, Hazel thought with a devious little smile tugging at her lips, if nature marooned them together and took her course, so be it. She suspected one thing for sure: knowing those two, they would not be coming down out of those mountains as ''just friends.''

No middle way for this cowboy and belle. Either they'd return madly in love or at each other's throats.

Nine

About an hour before dark, A.J. selected the spot for their second trail camp. It was a little bench of rocky ground beside a small spring that frothed up from a cluster of boulders.

They were well above the tree line now, although, according to Hazel's map, still well below Eagle Pass. The air had become noticeably thinner—all afternoon they had been forced to spell the horses more and more often.

Perhaps that thin air, in part, accounted for Jacquelyn's present splitting headache. It hammered the back of her eyeballs with a vengeance as she wearily stripped the saddle and bridle from Roman Nose, preparing to curry the dried sweat off him.

"Damn! I ain't *even* believing this!"

A.J.'s angry voice, right behind her, made her start and drop the currycomb.

"Lookit that saddle sore you've rubbed into his flank! Can't you see that? Now you're keeping the cinch too damn tight. Loosen the girth, you little fool."

He strode over to his pile of gear, returned and practically threw a jar of gall salve at her.

"Out here," he told her, his jaw tightening, "no better word can be spoken of a person than to say he's careful with horses."

"All fine and noble. But even if he isn't careful with people?"

The hurt and accusation in her tone didn't seem to faze him one bit.

"In my experience," he replied, "a man careless with one is careless with the other."

"Oh, really? I beg to differ. *My* experience shows that a man is quite capable of treating horses better than he treats people."

"Ain't you persecuted, huh? Well, spare me the violins. I told you once already about the horses. You ain't back at the country club now with somebody to do all the hard work for you. Roman Nose is *your* responsibility. And so far you're doing a pretty poor job. I'm damned if I know why Hazel sent some sniveling miss on a trip like this, anyhow."

The resentment in his tone made it clear that the saddle sore was only a pretext for unloading on her. But she was in no mood to endure more of his abuse. She had an aching head, an aching behind, and she was sick of being jerked around by this conceited rodeo pimp.

"And *I'm* damned," she exploded in a return salvo, "if I know why she did, either! I came to experience a bit of history, not to endure your know-it-all harping and criticizing! It's browbeating, that's what it is! Just plain browbeating like my—"

She caught herself before she finished it. *Like my father does to my mother.*

Gathering herself, she said, "First you yell at me because the girth is too loose. Then you freak out because it's too tight. Every move I make, you've got some complaint about it. And I am *not* 'snivelling.' And what the hell did I ever do to you, anyway?''

As bad luck would have it, just as she added this last retort, tears sprang from her eyes. Overcome by emotion and exhaustion, she turned away from him and began rubbing salve on Roman Nose's sore flank.

He watched her from eyes shadowed beneath his brim. Finally he said, "This ain't personal."

"Oh, it's not?" she accused, refusing to look at him. "I suppose you'd treat one of your co-workers like this?"

"You're not a co-worker. You're a woman."

She finally looked at him, dismayed. "You can't mean that. You mean this is how you treat your rodeo bimbos?"

He released a quick, exasperated breath. "I don't take my women on a hard trip to Eagle Pass."

"Then forget I'm a woman," she demanded.

"Not likely," he murmured under his breath, his eyes darting away.

She stared at him for a long moment. "Why are you so uptight, A.J.? Why don't you take your rodeo bimbos up here? You clearly love these mountains—why not bring one of your girlfriends here?" Her mouth gave a cynical tug. "I bet I can guess why. Up here you'd have to see them as people."

"I see women as people. I sure see Hazel that way."

"Yes, you do. But the others are just 'fillies' to you. Why is that? Why, if you love women so much, haven't you settled down with one woman?"

"I don't need a girlfriend. I got lots of women." He was angry now by the flash in his eyes.

"But why not just one? Why not?" she insisted, her own anger cathartic.

"Damn you!" he snapped. "Because if I got plenty, then if one gets taken away, then—then—"

He turned away. Every muscle in his body seemed as tense as forged iron. He cursed. "Then I won't miss them."

She just stared at him; somehow she wondered if she hadn't unknowingly stumbled on to his Achilles' heel.

He shook his head and looked up as if for help. "You want to know why I don't take them up here? Because trying to figure out a woman is like trying to bite your own teeth."

"You don't know the secret, A.J. And the secret is, a woman's just like you. *I'm* just like you," she managed, unable to trust her voice further.

He walked away.

Oddly, though, their little confrontation seemed to act as a sort of pressure valve, at least for a brief time. A grudging, temporary peace ensued. By the time she had strapped a nose bag on Roman Nose and set up her tent, he had built up a cheery fire using wood he gathered on the lower slopes.

"Notice anything missing?" he commented in a civil tone when she approached the fire.

She listened for a moment as she searched for a flat rock so she could sit down. Then she realized that a familiar, constant crackle had ceased.

"No insect noise," she replied.

"Right. We're too high up now for most of 'em."

"Feels like it," she said, pulling on a long-sleeved knit sweater.

She stared at him in the flickering firelight as he removed his tight boots.

"You were right about needing heels to hold the stirrups securely," she finally confessed to him. "I'm working that into my story. Also the fact that your biggest laugh, so far, was when I went into the creek."

"I enjoyed it," he confessed, "but only because I also warned you plenty."

She nodded, amazed they were actually having a civil exchange.

A few minutes of peaceful silence ticked by while lone sparks escaped into the sky like fleeing fireflies. Every now and again she caught him glancing at her. For a few brief moments their gazes held, then she found she had to look away. Something in his stare was just too invasive, too heavy with implication. It unnerved her to ponder it when they were so far from civilization.

Weariness settled deep into her bones. She never thought she'd see the day when she was sleepy by 8:00 p.m.

Her eyelids began to take on weight. His quiet, calm voice prodded her awake.

"Full moon tonight. You quoted Jake in your last article. 'The full moon favors lovers and lunatics.' Which are we?"

So the man of action deigned to read her articles? Maybe just to see if he's mentioned, she told herself sarcastically.

"You mean there's a difference?" she commented.

He chuckled. "Hazel said you had a good sense of humor. Maybe she was right."

"Too bad, though, I'm such a spoiled brat, right?"

"That's the way of it," he agreed.

She rose to her feet.

He followed.

"Well, good night, Mr. Clayburn."

He stood watching her. That strange frisson went down her spine again. She was so close to him, she could have reached out and touched his hard cheek.

"Good night, Miss Rousseaux," he rasped. His gaze lowered to her figure. He seemed to be thinking about something, and she was pretty sure it was the same thing on her mind.

His hands reached out and drew her into his chest. She couldn't breathe, nor did she struggle. He seemed like a drug at that moment, one she waited all her life to get a fix of.

A shrill whinny from one of the horses suddenly doused them like a fall into Crying Horse Stream. He pushed her away. Both animals were ground hitched, with picket pins and short ropes, about twenty feet away. The mustangs began bucking and jackknifing, trying to pull the pickets loose.

She felt her scalp crawl when he slid his rifle from its leather scabbard.

"What is it?" she asked as he ran to the horses, quickly gentling both animals by speaking low and close to their ears.

He jacked a round into the rifle chamber. The sound echoed ominously in the quiet darkness.

"I'd say they've caught a whiff of bear," he explained, his eyes scouring the surrounding darkness. "And pretty close by, too. Horses are scared to death of bears."

She stood up and walked over by the horses, out of the friendly glow of the fire. Like him, she too stared down the mountain slope. Shifting moon shadows gave a sinister cast to the landscape.

"Something's not right," he announced in a puzzled voice. "If it was winter, then bears this low wouldn't surprise me. They'll go right into a town when they wake up hungry enough. But in summer? These mountain bears will almost always stick to the highest ground they can so's to avoid men. They've learned about hunters and guns."

"So why would one be this low?"

"Tell you what," he said earnestly. "If this one stops by for a chat, I'll ask it."

"C'mon, humor me. One point of my article is my education along the trail. What drives bears lower besides hunger?"

"Could be there's people up above," he speculated. "Rock climbers come up here, and sometimes researchers from the university. Or maybe there's some rough weather making up."

"The horses have calmed down now," she pointed out.

"Appears so," he agreed, lowering the muzzle of his rifle. "Anyhow, I'm turning in. G'night."

She stood and watched him replace the rifle in the scabbard. Then he resolutely ignored her to roll out his sleeping bag.

Feeling strangely devastated, she went to her tent and double-checked it, making sure that the entrance was zipped tightly closed. She had just burrowed into her sleeping bag when his taunting voice reached her from the other side of the dying fire.

"I'll try to warm my hands up before I search your sleeping bag in the morning," he promised.

"Good *night,* Mr. Clayburn," she called out testily. "I don't believe a search will be necessary."

"Maybe. Maybe not."

She deliberately ignored him, forcing herself to fall asleep. The last thing she was aware of, before sweet oblivion washed over her, was A.J.'s deep velvety voice soothing the still-jumpy mustangs.

It didn't take long, after she woke up on Thursday morning, for Jacquelyn to discover that last night's temporary truce with A.J. was over.

She had slept deeply, waking up feeling refreshed but still sore. Although the day's new sun was up, it hadn't yet burned off a morning mist. A thin powdering of frost covered the ground, reminding her how high they were climbing.

A.J. was nowhere in sight when she emerged from her tent, shivering. But the fire had been stoked to life, and the air was fragrant with the strong smell of "cowboy coffee."

She took down her tent, rolled it and her sleeping bag up, then tossed both bundles near her pile of riding gear. It was nippy this early, and each breath puffed white in the cool air.

Gathering clean clothes and a towel, she headed toward the nearby spring. It bubbled up in the midst of a clutch of huge boulders, only a few feet in diameter, but pure, delicious water. And the boulders afforded some natural privacy.

She was still a few yards away when she heard A.J. singing in a low voice, "'Buffalo gal, won't you come out tonight…come out tonight…come out tonight?'"

She rounded the first big boulder and spotted him. His back turned toward her as he washed in the little pool. He was completely naked in the water, splashing it over his head despite the chill air.

Once she had read somewhere that good rodeo riders developed strong physiques from the constant tensing and flexing required to stay in the saddle. But she hadn't expected the strong, defined muscles now rippling across his back and shoulders like taut steel cables. Nor the smooth, tight mounds of his buttocks that crowned a pair of tall, strong hairsprinkled legs.

He had the body of an Olympian.

She stood dazzled, watching him, aware once again that her body was betraying her. A heat melted like wax between her thighs. Her breath grew shallow, her heart beat stronger.

I thought only men, she admonished herself, could divorce their desires from their emotions like this. *How* could she feel instantly turned on at the sight of a man so self-centered and arrogant, so blue-collar and crude and foreign to her experience?

Feeling guilty at her chance voyeurism, she forced herself to go back to camp. But then he spun around and caught her.

Mortified, she stood frozen like a deer in the headlights.

Cupping his endowment, impressive even in the cold water, he flashed the familiar sarcastic grin. "Morning, peeping Jack!" he called out in a hail-fellow voice.

"I'm s-sorry. Really, I was not 'peeping,'" she protested, heat rising into her face.

"Why go away frustrated, m'heart? If you'd like, you can come join me." He threatened to remove the cup of his hands.

She was suddenly so embarrassed that she actually trembled. "In your dreams, cowboy."

"Dreams?" He laughed as if the word were a punch line. "Now me, I'm the kinda man, *if* I've got a dream I turn it into a reality. But don't get your hopes up, Jack, 'cuz I don't dream all that much about princesses like you. I like my girls earthy and fun."

Without him knowing it, his words hit her heart like an arrow to a bull's-eye. Wounded, she retaliated. "Sure, you don't want a woman like me. I don't have enough silicone in my bra and feathers in my head—just what a man like you deserves.''

He laughed.

She turned to leave him. He pulled on his jeans and followed her.

When he took her arm, the serious expression on his face jolted her. Her heart skipped a beat, then adrenaline and something more kicked into her veins.

She refused to admit to sexual attraction. Not here. Not with him and his stupid, cutting insults.

But something thrummed in her body, heating her, even when the hand on her arm was cold from the water.

And, oh, how she had wanted to see him all naked. To see what other women had had for their pleasure.

He pulled her toward him, closing the distance between them. His lips twisted in a secret smile. She swore he was testing her.

Her gaze held his. Defiantly she matched him moment for moment. It was a standoff. There was no telling whose will would prove the stronger. Until he made the final move.

His eyes still on her, he lowered his mouth.

Her instincts surged; she knew she should have turned her head away. But she didn't. She took his kiss with all the greed of a woman starved, of an ice princess desperate to thaw. He thrust his tongue into her mouth, and she opened hers even more, letting him in, no, willing him into the smooth, pink, wet cavern of her mouth.

Damp and hard, his arousal pressed against her. Immediately she regretted her weakness. She pulled away and pressed her hand against her burning mouth.

''Look at that,'' he marveled, his voice low and harsh. ''You're just a flesh-and-blood woman after all.''

She refused to look at him, refused to acknowledge his need, his arousal and her own reaction to it. ''I don't need you to tell me that,'' she whispered, unshed tears stinging in her eyes. "I know it better than anyone.''

Closing her eyes, she felt as if she had just danced her soul out in front of him.

He was silent for a long time. Without another word, he brushed past her. He sauntered away as if the moment had never occurred.

But it had, and they both knew it.

Jacquelyn was already primed for a bad mood even before they broke camp and resumed their ride toward Eagle Pass and Bridger's Summit beyond it. A.J., as usual, rode in the lead. Even looking at him from behind on horseback, she realized she couldn't shake the picture of him by the spring, naked, with rippling muscles.

At one point, perhaps an hour after they rode out, he pivoted around in his saddle. He bored those direct eyes of his right through her.

"Rock slide country up ahead,'' he informed her. "See all those traprock shelfs and outcroppings above us? Some are unstable. Quit building sand castles in your head and pay attention. You've got to stay aware up here.''

"Now you're a mind reader?'' she riposted. "How do you know I'm *not* paying attention?''

"Same way I know a plugged nickel has a hole in it. Just do what I tell you.''

"*Ja, mein herr!*'' she added a *sieg heil*, raising her right arm in a Third Reich salute.

He smiled darkly. "You'll call me worse than a Nazi before this little trip is in the books,'' he assured her. "And you try daydreaming on Devil's Slope, the trip *will* be over—for you.''

But despite his threatening and infuriating manner, she admitted to herself that his warning was due. She *was* tuning out and perhaps dangerously so.

However, she couldn't help herself. For various reasons

her mood was fluctuating between confusion and exhilaration. As it seized her in its grip, she was less and less able to stay alert and attuned to danger.

The magnificent view was a distraction all its own. From their elevation, she could see as far north as the Canadian Rockies, as far east as the North Dakota plains, as far south as the sprawling grasslands of eastern Wyoming. The grandeur of nature *should* equal grandeur of feeling.

But now was not the time. Instead, she let the pictures pile up inside her head, ignoring them. Nor did she any longer feel motivated to narrate impressions into her pocket recorder.

A.J.'s horse abruptly stopped on its own. The mustang's head came up, and it pricked its ears forward.

"Hold it," he called back, raising one hand to halt her.

"What is it?"

"Ask my horse, not me. He's the one on alert."

She watched A.J.'s slitted eyes carefully study the ridge all around them. "Might be our bear is still around," he said as he started his horse forward again. "Be careful. They can attack quick if surprised, especially a she-bear with cubs."

Even this threat, however, failed to penetrate the gloomy depths into which she felt herself steadily sinking. Indeed, the higher they rode, the lower she sank.

It wasn't by choice. It was simply the stark, unavoidable contrast between the past and the present; between the account of pioneer Jake, with his overpowering love of his new bride, and the lovelorn reality of her own life; between princesses and real women who embraced life with all its earthy pleasures.

It seemed so clear to her now, so devastatingly sure that such a love, such a sense of belonging as those lovers found in Mystery, were beyond her grasp.

And what did she have instead, she of the golden spoon and limitless opportunities? Right now she was growing increasingly dependent on the very man whom she desired more and more fervently to be away from.

Lost deep in such unpleasant thoughts, she fulfilled A.J.'s warning—she was caught completely off guard when trouble literally reared its head.

A.J.'s horse rose up, forelegs kicking savagely as A.J. fought to control him on the narrow, steep trail. Jacquelyn almost flew from the saddle when Roman Nose crow-hopped sideways, almost tumbling down the steep face of the mountain.

She heard the savage roar of the infuriated bear up ahead even before she spotted the animal. A.J. yanked his horse around, getting its nose out of the wind to quell its panic.

"Ride down our back trail!" he shouted at her. "*Now*, dammit!"

He stabbed both heels hard into his horse's flanks, grabbing Roman Nose by the bridle as he flashed past. She saw him yank the rifle from its saddle scabbard. Then, a heartbeat later, she saw the massive brown bear charging straight toward her flank, its huge fangs exposed for the kill.

Ten

It all happened in mere seconds. Yet to Jacquelyn it had a dream-time slowness to it, as if it were happening underwater.

She was too frightened to scream. As the huge, dusty, scarred animal lumbered closer, a shock wave of immobilizing fear slammed into her.

Her situation was precarious. Roman Nose had sidestepped off the narrow trail. A.J. tugged mightily at his bridle, trying to keep the terrified mustang under control on the steep slope.

However, A.J. also had to contend with his own spooked horse. As Roman Nose regained the trail, A.J.'s horse flew into total panic at the sight of the charging brown bear.

"Hang on!" he shouted to her as his mustang reared straight up on its hind legs, whickering in fright.

A.J., still holding Roman Nose's bridle, was almost pulled off his own horse. Jacquelyn, meantime, scrambled frantically to secure a good hold. But gravity was against her at a bad angle. One foot slipped from the stirrup, and in an instant she fell to the ground.

"The hell are you doing?" he demanded as if she'd planned the fall just to irk him.

As Roman Nose escaped down the mountain trail and the agitated bear hurtled even nearer, A.J. gave up trying to gentle his mount. There was no time for it. He leaped to the ground, slapped his horse hard on the rump, then jerked a still-shaken Jacquelyn roughly to her feet.

"Only for Hazel, you little fool," he muttered as he worked the lever of the rifle.

But he didn't aim for the bear. He fired into the air, the crack of detonation echoing along the slopes with diminishing force.

The sound didn't scare the determined bear off. But the creature halted momentarily, startled and unsure. It came up high on its hind legs, sampling the air.

"Don't stand there gawking like a ninny," he chastised his ashen-faced companion. "You skin that one while I chase the others over."

Jacquelyn was far too frightened to notice the humorous glint in A.J.'s eyes. "What?" she said uncertainly, her face stupid from fear. "What, *skin* it?"

"I'm kidding. Get back down the trail. *Get,* you damned idiot! It's a she-bear, thinks we mean to hurt or steal her cubs!"

He gave Jacquelyn a hard push in the direction the horses had fled. Even as she finally overcame her fear and started down the trail, the bear emitted a deep-chested roar and resumed its charge.

A.J. was right on her heels as Jacquelyn stumbled down the path. She heard the rifle speak again, but this time the bear seemed unfazed. Jacquelyn could hear it pounding ever closer, making little grunting noises that made her scalp tighten. She could even hear the sound of fabric tearing as the creature swiped at A.J.'s back.

"My God, A.J.!" she managed between heaving breaths. "Can't you shoot it?"

"For what?" he flung back. "Protecting her young? Quit whining and keep going! If we get out of her territory, she'll stay with her cubs and leave us."

Jacquelyn tried very hard not to think what might happen if she fell along the particular stretch they scrambled down. The ridge was steep. She could glance just to her right and below, where sheer cliffs curtain-folded away into steep gorges. Places so deep the sun never even reached the bottom at high noon.

She heard A.J. stop, though the bear still charged them. Was he finally going to shoot her? Despite not wanting to witness the kill, her fear and curiosity made her look over her shoulder.

She stopped in her tracks, not believing what she was in fact witnessing.

A.J.'s rifle lay on the ground beside him. He had stretched his six-foot, two-inch frame out to its full height by rising up on tiptoes. He exaggerated the effect by raising both arms high overhead, his jacket flapping alongside him like giant wings.

The bear, like Jacquelyn, had no idea at first what to make of this bizarre spectacle. A.J. further astonished both of them by suddenly emitting a deep *woof* noise that combined a bark with a growl. Not a bad imitation, she realized, of the bear.

"Bears don't see so good," he told her in a low voice. "And I'm downwind, so she can't smell me. Maybe if she thinks I'm another bear, she'll respect my territory and leave with her cubs."

After a tense ten seconds or so, the bear abruptly turned and dashed back up the trail.

"Well," A.J. decided, extracting the bullet from the rifle's chamber, "we best head back down the mountain and find our horses. Could be a hike, scared as they were. If you could just stay in the damned saddle…"

"Me? Roman Nose practically did a backward somersault."

"Yeah, so what? Don't matter if he chins the moon. It's your job to hang on. Damn near got both of us killed. And now we'll waste good time flushing out our horses. This means we set out even earlier in the morning."

"Earlier?" she exclaimed. "If we'd left any earlier this morning, it would've been yesterday."

He just held up a hand, tired of it. By now he was striding quickly down the trail, Jacquelyn practically trotting to keep up with his long legs. She kept looking behind them to make sure the bear wasn't just tricking them. Blood still pounded in her temples from the shock of their near miss.

"I was sure you'd shoot it," she told him. "I mean her—the bear."

He replied without looking at her. "Obviously you would've. S'matter, you trigger-happy?"

"I admit I would have tried to shoot it," she confessed. "But only because I was so scared. Still, I'm sure I would've missed and just really made her angry."

"Then you're double useless up here," he said with scathing bluntness. "Too eager to kill, yet inadequate to the task."

"'Eager!'" she bristled. "Now I'm a killer on your say-so? You manage to turn everything into an insult or a crime, don't you?"

Instantly she regretted her remark. Not what she had said, but her little-girl-hurting tone. It made her angry at herself to show him she needed his approval.

"You want affection," he growled at her, "get a dog. Hazel didn't ask me to build up your self-esteem, just run you ragged in the mountains."

"Well, you're doing a pretty damned good job of that!" she flung at him.

Her comment made him grin. He finally looked at her. "Step it out, Peeping Jack. We're burning daylight."

* * *

By the time they finally caught up with their horses, they had descended well down into the tree-covered slopes again.

"No point riding on now," A.J. grumbled as he gauged the amount of light left in the sky. "We've lost all our wood, anyway, and I'll need to gather more. We'll camp right here."

"What'll we do for water?" she asked as she studied the little pine copse where they'd found the horses grazing.

"We're okay for tonight. Tomorrow we'll just watch where the closest birds go at dawn. They always drink at daybreak."

He left to forage for firewood while she tended to the horses. The huge adrenaline high of the bear incident was now followed by a zooming crash of her emotions. Her despair had returned with a vengeance.

Hazel was right, she decided. The trip *was* a benchmark event in her young life. It was throwing into stark relief the harsh fact that she was alone, cut off, walled off.

Suddenly her throat closed so tight it hurt. Hot tears welled up from her eyes. Afraid A.J. would return and catch her, she sought out a lonely spot behind a tangled deadfall far away from camp. And there she dug up the grave of her hopes and buried them all anew.

"Was hoping the bear got you," the cowboy greeted her when she returned to camp. His tone was gruffly cordial.

"Sorry to disappoint you," she volleyed back. "Maybe you'll get rid of me on Devil's Slope."

He laughed.

Trouble's coming, she warned herself as she looked at him. She was becoming fragile; he was becoming friendly. I'll pay, she thought blackly as she sat in front of the fire to warm herself.

Night settled down on the mountains like a dark blanket. The campfire was going strong.

"What's that...interesting smell?" she finally asked.

He pointed to a skinned rabbit roasting on a greenwood

Here's a  HOT offer for you!

Get set for a sizzling summer read...

with **2 FREE ROMANCE BOOKS** and a **FREE MYSTERY GIFT!**

NO CATCH! NO OBLIGATION TO BUY!

Simply complete and return this card and you'll get **2 FREE BOOKS** and **A FREE GIFT** – yours to keep!

Visit us online at www.eHarlequin.com

- The first shipment is yours to keep, **absolutely free!**
- Enjoy the convenience of Silhouette Desire® books delivered right to your door, before they're available in stores!
- Take advantage of special low pricing for **Reader Service Members only!**
- After receiving your free books we hope you'll want to remain a subscriber. But the choice is always yours—to continue or cancel, any time at all! So why not take us up on this fabulous invitation, with no risk of any kind. You'll be glad you did!

326 SDL C26Q

225 SDL C26L
(S-D-OS-06/00)

▼ DETACH HERE AND MAIL CARD TODAY! ▼

Name:	
(Please Print)	
Address:	Apt.#:
City:	
State/Prov.:	Zip/ Postal Code:

Offer limited to one per household and not valid to current Silhouette Desire® subscribers.
All orders subject to approval. © 1998 HARLEQUIN ENTERPRISES LTD. ® & TM are trademarks owned by Harlequin Books S.A. used under license.

The Silhouette Reader Service™ —Here's how it works:

Accepting your 2 free books and gift places you under no obligation to buy anything. You may keep the books and gift and return the shipping statement marked "cancel." If you do not cancel, about a month later we'll send you 6 additional novels and bill you just $3.34 each in the U.S., or $3.74 each in Canada, plus 25¢ delivery per book and applicable taxes if any.* That's the complete price and — compared to cover prices of $3.99 each in the U.S. and $4.50 each in Canada — it's quite a bargain! You may cancel at any time, but if you choose to continue, every month we'll send you 6 more books, which you may either purchase at the discount price or return to us and cancel your subscription.

*Terms and prices subject to change without notice. Sales tax applicable in N.Y. Canadian residents will be charged applicable provincial taxes and GST.

If offer card is missing write to: Silhouette Reader Service, 3010 Walden Ave., P.O. Box 1867, Buffalo, NY 14240-1867

BUSINESS REPLY MAIL
FIRST-CLASS MAIL   PERMIT NO. 717   BUFFALO, NY

POSTAGE WILL BE PAID BY ADDRESSEE

SILHOUETTE READER SERVICE
3010 WALDEN AVE
PO BOX 1867
BUFFALO NY 14240-9952

NO POSTAGE
NECESSARY
IF MAILED
IN THE
UNITED STATES

spit over the fire. "Caught it with a snare," he informed her. "That's how Jake took care of his supper more than once up here. Didn't have to shoot his gun and announce his position."

"I'm sure it's tasty. But I think I'll settle for a granola bar and an apple," she demured.

He stared at her. All he said was, "Leaves more for me."

She was able to set up her pup tent like an old pro by now. When she finished, she noticed that he was gingerly removing his flannel shirt. She spotted blood spatters on the back of it, and a little prickle of alarm went through her.

"You're hurt," she said, crossing to the spot where he straddled a log beside the fire.

"Ahh, it's small potatoes," he assured her. "Mama bear swiped me once up on the slope, but it wasn't deep."

"You let that bear get so close?"

"Let? She didn't exactly require my permission."

She moved around behind him. Several long scratches covered the hard ridge of muscle across his upper back.

"You're right, they're not deep," she agreed, her tone relieved. "But they really should be disinfected."

A.J., looking a little sheepish, held up a brown plastic bottle. "I know Jake didn't have hydrogen peroxide. He used carbolic acid, which hurt like hellfire and stank like hair burning."

"Let me help you. You can't reach them."

She took the bottle from him and returned to her tent to get a little first-aid kit she had brought along.

"You better lie down," she suggested when she returned, "or it'll all just run off too quick."

He unrolled his sleeping bag and stretched out on his stomach. She took over the log he deserted. She soaked a cotton ball in peroxide and sponged his back with it. In the coppery firelight, the lines and ridges of his muscles seemed sculpted. She had a hard time concentrating on her ministrations when she remembered how his backside looked without the jeans.

She taped gauze over the scratches, so his shirt wouldn't irritate them. While she was applying the last strip of adhesive tape, a light rain began slapping down. She started hurrying up.

"Don't bother rushing, won't be enough to get us wet," he assured her in a sleepy, relaxed voice. "Just enough to settle the dust."

"I take it this isn't that bad weather you've mentioned?"

"Not hardly." But he said no more on that subject.

"Summer rain back in Georgia," she observed, "always sounds softer and prettier because of the leaves. Same here."

Hardly feeling a drop, thanks to overhead boughs, she sat in silence for a few minutes, listening to the whispering patter. As he had predicted, it was over quickly. Afterward, the quiet was so complete she could hear the trees drip.

She had finished her task. There was no excuse to stay around. But then she had an idea.

"You know what?" she told him. "I just realized. Here I am, traveling in the mountains with one of Montana's favorite celebrities. And I haven't even got you on tape yet. Okay if I interview you for a bit?"

"I guess, but none of them boxers-or-briefs questions, okay?"

"Your secret is safe with me. Although no doubt plenty of women already know that answer."

"God bless 'em all in several languages," he added piously as she went to get her pocket recorder. By the time she returned, he was sitting up again, buttoning on a clean shirt against the night's gathering chill.

"So tell me, as a lifelong resident of Mystery Valley—has it changed that much during your lifetime?"

"Too much. Though it's still the finest valley in Montana. When I was a kid, Mystery had only one hotel, and that one the size of a packing crate. Now look. Got us a Ramada Inn, a Hampton House, even a Motel 6 out on Crawford Road. Might be a KOA campground coming, too."

Not to mention an upscale tourist suburb in the pipeline, Jacquelyn thought. She felt a lance of guilt as she recalled her father's plans for "site development" in Mystery Valley and elsewhere.

Eager to change the subject, she asked, "Why'd your people come out West originally? To farm or raise cattle?"

"Neither one, actually. See, my great-granddaddy Horace Clayburn had to flee out West from the law in Missouri."

"What'd he do?"

"Among other charges they made public, he stole a steamboat."

She studied his hard impassive face. Bright firelight reflected rubies in his eyes. But she detected none of the usual irony in his strong, expressive lips.

"Really?" she said, impressed and fascinated. "He actually took a steamboat?"

He nodded. "His only mistake was going back for the river. They hanged him."

Suddenly feeling foolish in a good-natured way, she shared a rare moment of laughter with him as he reeled her in. She thumbed off the recorder.

"Since you got all that on tape," he added, "I'll expect to see it in print. That's a clan joke among us Clayburns."

"You're not my editor, but don't worry. I'll use it. Classic example of a greenhorn—me—falling for a Western tall tale."

They both fell silent, listening to the peaceful sounds of night settling in. Pine pitch sizzled in the hot fire; wind whispered in the treetops; now and then one of the horses snuffled.

She looked at him at the precise moment he looked at her. Their eyes met, held, and suddenly the moment was oddly intimate.

Her throat was dry. She swallowed.

"This trip is getting interesting, isn't it?" he said.

Feeling insecure somehow, she stood up, brushing bits of

bark from her jeans. "I guess my interview has gone as far as it can go," she announced with forced lightness.

He smiled a little. "Pretty near," he agreed, watching her.

"Well...good night." She headed to her tent.

"Jacquelyn."

She drew up, surprised. It was the first time she could recall his using her first name.

Slowly she turned around to look at him. In the burnished firelight, his rugged, handsome features seemed to capture the essential ideal of "the Western man."

"Yes?" she inquired carefully, fearful about what he might say next, do next.

"We'll be starting early in the morning. Got to make up lost time," he announced, looking away to the fire.

She stared at him for a long moment, sure he'd been about to say something else. But then, like taunting the grizzly, she decided retreat was the most prudent action.

Without comment she crawled into her cold tent and zipped up her sleeping bag. She tried most of the night to get some sleep but sleep evaded her as her thoughts returned again and again to the naked cowboy in the spring, the sound of her name upon his lips and what it all might mean.

Eleven

She's man wary, A.J. told himself as he watched Jacquelyn duck into her tent. Just like those mustangs were when I first penned them.

Something had happened to her back East. Hazel didn't mention any details, nor did he care to know any. But the old girl did hint that Jacquelyn Rousseaux had recently experienced a "romantic misfortune."

Too bad for her, A.J. thought with a flare-up of resentment. Did she think *she* was so special bees wouldn't sting her? What, love was supposed to go easy on her because she was Big Daddy's rich little belle?

He stirred himself to life, rising to throw a few more good-size limbs onto the crackling fire. Mindful their bear friend might yet pass this way, he wanted plenty of flames through the night.

When he sat back down, his thoughts once more trailed to the woman in the tent. He would bet she'd figured he would be the proverbial putty in her female hands—just some redneck hick from the backwater. Well, it served her right how hard he'd been on her. She had to learn that A. J. Clayburn didn't lick salt from *any* woman's hand.

Then again, an inner voice niggled at him, maybe Hazel's instincts were sound. The girl was holding up better than he'd ever thought she could. He reluctantly had to admit it. She *did* have a lot of pluck to go along with those good looks and that shapely body. Sure, she screwed up plenty. Sure she was green. But she was smart, and she never made the same mistake twice. That was more than he could say for a few of the men on his payroll.

With the fire well stoked, he crossed the camp clearing to check on the horses. At the first sound of his movement, her muffled voice called out fearfully, "Who's that?"

"Just us angry bears. Go to sleep."

"What's wrong? Did you hear something?"

He grinned, shaking his head in the dark. "No need to get spooked. I'm just checking on the horses."

With a fast *zwip* sound, she opened the fly of her tent and stepped outside to watch him with wary suspicion. He was only a shadowy outline at the very edge of the firelight.

"The horses are fine," she assured him, her voice defensive.

"You been taking good care of them," he acknowledged. "I'm not faulting you. Even Roman Nose's saddle gall is better."

His grin widened as he recalled a scene from earlier, before dark set in. He had seen her using her fingernail file to painstakingly probe out a stone too small for the hoof pick. If the thing had lodged in the animal's hoof and been neglected, it could cause a crack to work its way up the coronet and eventually lame the horse. She *did* have some sound horsemanship behind her.

"I'm just gonna fill their nose bags again," he explained. "We'll be leaving earlier and moving faster than usual to make up lost time. Plus we'll have Devil's Slope to cross. It's rough on riders, but it's double rough on the horses.''

"Yes," she said, her voice distrustful. "You've already reminded me a dozen times about Devil's Slope. And I have to tell you that I read Jake's diary entry about it. He referred to it as only 'an annoyance.' Maybe he didn't scare as easily as you do?''

"An annoyance," he repeated. "And when Jake caught a Confederate bullet in his left lung at Gettysburg, *that* was a 'flesh wound.' You ain't Jake McCallum.''

She flounced back into her tent without comment and again sealed herself off from him—a favorite pastime of hers, he thought.

He laughed outright as he scooped a mixture of corn and oats into the canvas nose bags. When he considered how soft her usual routine was, she *was* hanging in there like a champ. Never mind how much he despised her elitist assumptions and what her family stood for, the rodeo artist within him greatly admired her tenacity for simply hanging on and enduring.

For the first time he wondered if he had confused Eric Rousseaux with Jacquelyn. It finally occured to him that he might be punishing the daughter for the sins of the father—and nothing in the highly vaunted Code of the West allowed a man to be that unfair. You were supposed to judge each person on their own merits.

And she was holding up pretty good. If he didn't know better, he mused, he would almost suspect the girl was true pioneer stock.

His moment of benevolence passed quickly, however. He sure as hell didn't want to get his emotions mixed up with her. She wasn't the acrylic-nailed, vapid-gazed rodeo groupie who loved a one night stand. This woman would ask for something more—something he didn't know if he could ever give. To fall in love meant vulnerability. And all his life he'd chosen the toughest broncs just to prove he had no vulnerability. No, he wasn't going to fall in love with no fool woman. He wasn't going to take the risk. People had a way of leaving him when he did that. No matter how tough he was, he knew deep inside he wasn't tough enough to take it again like the death of his parents had given it to him.

So that beauty with the sea-green eyes wasn't going to get under his skin. They still had Devil's Slope to ride out. She would break yet, he predicted as he returned to his bedroll. He'd seen it all before on greenhorns. She'll get scared, and then she'll turn on him like a rabid animal and show her true colors: money-green, snob-purple, and chicken-yellow.

They hit the trail at the ungodly hour of 4:00 a.m. Jacquelyn quickly realized the horses were in a far better mood than she was.

She searched her journalistic vocabulary for the right verb to describe their arduous progress for the next eight hours. She finally settled for *slogged*. And despite her determination, fear began to poke at her mind long before they reached Devil's Slope.

"Falling rocks," A.J. explained, pointing up the scarred face of the mountain, "form furrows like that one right in front of us. The French trappers hereabouts called them *couloirs*. You have to be careful in them. The sides are stable, but the middle part is stone swept. That furrow you're looking at now is easy climbing, at first. But it'll become Devil's Slope about one hour farther up."

It was only noon. But her muscles ached and trembled from the rigors of the ascent that brought them back above the trees. They had stopped briefly to rest the horses and gnaw on thick, gnarled hunks of beef jerky.

"It's getting a lot colder," she commented as she dug another pullover out of her duffel. "Windier, too."

Even as she spoke, a sudden wind gust almost seized A.J.'s hat.

"Sure it is. We're climbing higher," was all he said.

However, that same wind was also piling dark clouds on the horizon like boulders. He hadn't bothered mentioning it to her, but his eyes seemed to be cloaking worry. Besides the terrain, his face was another thing that had her unsettled.

"The main thing you got to remember on loose rocks," he lectured her as they prepared to push on, "is smooth weight transfer. If you do it right, you can put a lot of weight on loose rock. But don't jerk your horse or you'll risk sliding."

She started to tilt her canteen to her lips for a drink. His iron grip stopped her hand.

"Never drink when you're sweating. Wait till you cool off. Otherwise it'll just evaporate before it can do your body any good." He looked down at her, and for some reason seemed to be giving her body a very frank appraisal just at that moment—as if he was curious about exactly where she was sweating. When she caught him staring, he added hastily, "And we can't order room service for a Perrier way up here, so conserve your water."

She almost wanted to smile. "Be careful, there. You actually sounded considerate for a moment. You're not getting all female and 'mushy' on me, are you, Daniel Boone?"

"Don't worry," he promised her, pushing his horse forward. "If I was, I'll make up for it with meanness later."

She glanced up the long, narrow, unstable furrow they were about to start climbing. Fear lay heavy in her stomach like a ball of ice. If all else failed for her, there was always bluff and bluster. She thrust her chin out with determination.

He seemed to sense her fear and false bravado. "Ready?" he asked.

"Ready when you are, Mr. Clayburn," she told him defiantly.

His sarcastic lips twisting, he went ahead, intoning in a solemn voice that nonetheless mocked her, "Our Father, who art in heaven…"

* * *

A.J. was right about the *couloir:* its sloping sides were fairly stable—at first. Although Roman Nose occasionally slid on smooth stone, the ground underfoot was solid and stable.

Because of the danger to the second rider in a single-file ascent, each of them took a separate side of the furrow. Jacquelyn took great care to keep Roman Nose from wandering too close to the unstable middle.

Too soon, however, the going got a lot rougher. Now even the far edges of the *couloir* were littered with broken talus and loose volcanic scree.

"Just slack your reins," he called over. "Give your horse his head and let him pick his own way."

She did as ordered, too scared at the moment to resent yet one more surly command. But it felt strange to be completely passive and useless, dependent on a half-wild mustang for her life.

Gradually A.J.'s horse worked its way higher up than Roman Nose. She watched him draw rein, waiting for her to catch up on her side.

"Good thing you buffed your nails, huh?" he called out, adding a mocking laugh.

He stood up in the stirrups to see up the slope better. In that one offguard moment, the mountainside began to move. In the sliding rock, his horse lost his footing. The animal fell to his knees and scrambled to get back on all fours. Caught off balance, A.J. had no time to react. He was tossed from the saddle like a doll from a dog's mouth. She saw him hit the slope, bounce once, then lie ominously still.

"A.J.! A.J., are you all right?"

But the real trouble was still shaping up. As A.J.'s panicked horse got his footing and took off, the animal escaped higher and higher, sending another shower of debris sliding down toward him. So far nothing big had struck, but the rock slide was gathering size and force as the horse clambered higher.

"A.J.!"

Thank God! At least he was struggling to sit up, so he wasn't seriously hurt. He tried to stand, but his knees seemed to have come unhinged. She saw how glazed and unfocused his eyes were and realized he'd struck his head.

With a crashing roar that made her gasp, a huge, heavy rock smashed down the slope only a few yards from him. More detritus was thundering down on him, and he couldn't possibly survive another thirty seconds in that deadly slide.

In that moment, without willing it to happen, her reflexes and years of riding took over.

Heedless of the danger, she reined sharp left and squeezed Roman Nose's shoulders with her calves. The game little horse leaped right into the unstable moraine and talus at the center of the furrow.

Everything she had ever learned in show jumping came into instant focus in the next critical moments. Balance, grace, control and precise, split-second decisions that meant life or death. All guided her now as they had over hurdles and around obstacles.

She had to ride a wild, crinkum-crankum pattern to avoid the worst spots. The deft mustang responded precisely to each tug of the reins, her will becoming his. But when, by some miracle, she actually cleared the unstable center, she had a full-blown rock slide to avoid on the other side.

"A.J.!" she shouted above the train-yard roar of falling debris. "A.J., can you hear me?"

He had managed to get to his knees—she could see him through the gathering dust cloud. But he was still groggy and out of it.

Somehow, assisted by fear strength, she helped him onto the horse, then got mounted heself without either of them being crushed. But now she had to get back across to her side with his extra weight to endanger them.

With one hand stretched awkwardly behind her to steady him, she clutched the reins in the other. Roman Nose began picking his way back across the rock-swept center of the *couloir.*

Unfortunately, in all the dust and racket and confusion, she wasn't able to pick the same safe route she followed coming over. They were perhaps halfway across when the slope under Roman Nose turned deadly. They started sliding.

Her heart leaped into her throat. She realized the section of the furrow was almost all unstable. Roman Nose managed to heave himself up onto a small section of stable rock. But now, she realized with a sinking feeling, they were virtually marooned on a tiny island.

She could clearly see the stable slope now, only a few tempting yards away. Could they jump it? It was unlikely, what with this double load on such a small horse. And so little room to build up any speed.

But what other choice did she have, with half the mountain tumbling down around them?

"Hold on, A.J.!" she shouted, not knowing if he could understand her. "Gee up, Roman Nose!" she added, slapping the mustang's neck and squeezing her knees. "Hiii-*ya!*"

Again her training took over. She assumed the classic jump position, lowering herself in the saddle with her torso forward. Bent low over Roman Nose's neck, she spoke urgently to him, assuring him he could make the jump.

Now!

With fine-tuned timing, she slacked the reins and let Roman Nose get his head down for the jump. They went airborne, then landed hard on solid ground. A.J. almost slid off on impact, but somehow managed to stay on.

For a moment, realizing what she had just accomplished, she began to tremble with pent-up emotion. But she quickly realized they were far from safe yet. She still had to get them the rest of the way across Devil's Slope. On her own.

A.J., a huge blue-black bruise swelling his left temple, slowly regained strength and awareness as they progressed up the dangerous slope. By now the wind gusts were so cold that she shivered despite several layers of clothing. And although it was still only the middle of the afternoon, the sky had grown as dark as twilight.

He said little during the ascent. They finally reached the stable ground above Devil's Slope, and his mustang stood calmly waiting for them.

He had regained his strength by now and swung down to the ground easily. Then he surprised her by reaching up to help her down. Those probing searchlight eyes of his looked at her differently somehow. With less derision.

"National Velvet saves the Rodeo King. That was a hell of a jump you and Roman Nose made back there," he told her. "Maybe I better look into this English riding, huh?"

She couldn't believe it. The insufferably egotistic A. J. Clayburn actually had some humility in his tone. She studied him, sure she could also detect a tone of wounded male vanity. He praised her now, but she might yet have to pay for that rescue. It wouldn't surprise her at all.

"I just can't imagine you in a hunting jacket," she assured him, shivering against the raw knife-edge of the wind. "My God, it's getting c-cold!"

He nodded as he grabbed his saddle horn, then swung up into leather.

"You did a nice job on Devil's Slope." His eyes lifted to the rapidly gathering raft of black storm clouds. "But the waltz ain't over yet," he added grimly. "C'mon, let's hurry. Between this spot and Eagle Pass is some of the area's worst avalanche country—and we've got a skyload of snow about to fall on us."

Twelve

He was right: the "waltz" was far from over.

They were perhaps one hour beyond Devil's Slope when the heavens opened up on them with a vengeance. A thick, damp, heavy snowfall was whipped into a blinding fury by unrelenting wind gusts.

There was no good place to take cover, so stopping was not an option. Fearful of separation as visibility decreased, A.J. tied a lead line to Roman Nose's bit ring.

"Cave up ahead a few hundred yards!" he shouted close to Jacquelyn's ear, his voice barely audible above the shrieking wind. "It's big enough that we all can take shelter!"

By now Jacquelyn couldn't see more than a few feet past the nose of her horse. But it was the cold that most tortured her Southern system, bone-numbing cold such as she had never before experienced. Even her soaking in Crying Horse Creek hadn't left her shivering like this.

But A.J.'s mental map proved reliable again. She gave silent thanks when he abruptly appeared again out of the white, windblown vastness. He pointed her off the trail, and within moments she had followed him into a large, wide cavern with a dry floor of rammed earth.

"Hobble your horse to the right of the entrance," he told her. "There's a little seep spring there if it ain't froze up yet."

She noticed his tone had definitely changed since the near miss on Devil's Slope. He still gave orders, but no longer in the voice of a sergeant to a worthless recruit.

"This place isn't on Hazel's map," she remarked as she secured Roman Nose, foreleg to rear, with short strips of rawhide.

"That's because Jake gave it wide berth," he confessed.

"Wide berth?" the reporter in her asked, stomping snow off her boots. "Why?"

"It was bad medicine. Mountain Utes used to entomb their dead here."

She cast a restive glance about them.

A.J., busy building a fire with the last of their wood, laughed. "Don't worry. Every last bone and bead has been stolen by artifact hunters."

She digested that depressing news, then crossed to the wide entrance. Clutching her elbows against the cold, she tried to see outside, but raging wind and driving snow formed a virtual whiteout.

"My God," she said, fear showing in her voice. "It's *terrible* out there. I can't believe it. What if we...I mean, but what if—"

"Just settle down," he said, fanning tiny flames larger with his hat. "This is Montana, girl. A little bad weather ain't nothing. Won't be long till you're safe and snug in the cabin on Bridger's Summit."

"From your lips to God's ears," she said softly, still glancing outside. "I can't believe it's August. Not looking at that."

"It's not August that matters, it's altitude and longitude.

But this weather now is just chicken-fixins. I got caught in a summer snowstorm up here back in '93. I survived by crawling inside a hollow log for a day and a half. The snow got so deep the rabbits suffocated in their burrows.'' He added with a grin, ''Man, did I have to pee when I finally crawled out.''

''You *knew* we could have weather like this? And you still went along with Hazel's idea?''

''Car wrecks happen, too. Should I quit driving?''

His tone scoffed at her. He had a point, and she let it go. It wasn't as though he knew this exact storm was coming, she reminded herself.

''Better get warm while you can,'' he called over to her. ''This is the last of our wood. I expected our next stop to be the cabin. Once this burns out, we stay cold until we can get to the summit.''

''Couldn't we just stay here?'' she suggested, again staring out into that white swirl. ''I mean, won't help be sent?''

''Help?'' He tossed back his head and laughed. ''Why? Lady, you do beat all. We ain't in no scrape yet.''

She glanced at the large knot forming on his head. ''But what about your concussion? You blacked out back there.''

''Nothing. Besides, even if we did need help, they can't get to us here. This place is God forgotten. We're on our own.''

She knelt beside the little fire, grateful for the sustaining heat as she held her hands over it. But the warmth did little to quell the fear, fatigue and depression that combined to sink her spirits.

A few minutes passed in silence while she brooded and watched the flames burn gradually lower. He said something, his voice nudging her back to the present.

''Pardon me?''

He sat directly across the fire from her, cross-legged like an Indian in the council lodge.

"I said, I'll bet you didn't tell your boyfriends back in Georgia about this little trip with me, huh?"

"Boy*friends?* Should I have put out a press release? You rodeo stars are the ones with harems."

"*Harems* is a stretch, but we do have our little fan clubs."

"Poor baby, stuck here with a steel magnolia when he's used to his lilting daisies…"

"I can bear up. I'm tough. You're the one seems to be moping. Like maybe you miss…somebody."

Yes, she thought with a pang behind her heart. *Some*body. But who? Who can warm up to the ice princess?

"I'm not moping," she finally told him, starting to shiver harder as the fire died down. "I'm just tired."

"If we want to repeat old Jake's experience, that means getting bone-deep tired. And bone-deep discouraged," he added, his tone actually kind, as if to rally her spirits.

Jake and Libbie, Jacquelyn thought with a little stab of resentment. Yes, what they had was real, all right. But theirs was a simpler, more sentimental age. And they were stronger people than she. What they seized was beyond her grasp.

The fire was nearly dead now, down to its last rubylike embers. Her entire body felt thoroughly chilled, and little warmth lingered in the drafty cavern. Beyond the entrance, blizzard-force winds shrieked like souls in torment.

She wasn't sure exactly when A.J. suddenly appeared at her side, unrolling his sleeping bag.

"Take your boots off," he instructed her. "Then crawl inside my bag. We're going to pool our warmth."

She started to shake her head.

"Look," he insisted, "believe me, I'm *not* making a pass at you. When I do that, I don't bother with tricks. But we could be in here for some time yet, and I'm damned if you're going to freeze to death on *my* watch. Hazel would skin me alive. Now stow the modesty and crawl in there."

She smiled weakly at the scolding in his tone. "Fine. Besides, we've got a dozen layers of clothing between us."

"So I'll be safe," he quipped. Before he climbed into the bag, he ducked outside and packed the coffeepot full of snow.

"Case the seep spring freezes," he explained as he wiggled into the sleeping bag with her.

She stared at him, no doubt with wariness in her eyes. The awkwardness was already beginning to wear off, however, when her teeth quit chattering. Already she was warmer. But he was so close. And yet so very warm. And the scent of him dark, male and enticing. Dangerous.

Her gaze caught sight of the bruise on A.J.'s temple—the legacy of his accident on Devil's Slope. She pushed herself up on one elbow to look at the injury, then scooped a little snow out of the coffeepot and held it gently against his bruise.

"How's that feel?" she asked.

"Nice."

She could feel his pulse throbbing against her fingers. Their eyes met, and suddenly she realized their mouths were well within kissing range. Her own pulse quickened.

The heat between them was literally palpable—the handful of snow melted like butter on a hot grill.

She lay back down, wondering what her next move should be. The etiquette of hypothermia was unclear. Did she sleep facing him to keep an eye on him, or did she put her back against his chest, and shut him out that way? She wasn't sure, and in the end she didn't make the choice. He merely grabbed her and pulled her back against his chest. Despite the brief pyrotechnics between them moments before, it was comfort and warmth she sought now, not erotic gratification. His masculine solidity was exactly what she needed with the backdrop of howling wind and blowing snow.

"That flower soap of yours smells nice," he muttered in a sleepy tone.

"What flower soap?"

"Then maybe just you smells nice," he said, starting to breathe evenly as sleep overtook him.

"Will this snow stop soon, do you think?" she asked.

But her words simply disappeared like stones down a deep well—he was asleep, his chest rising and falling like a slow bellows. The only answer she received came from the wind. It rose to a shrieking roar that drove swirling snow into the cavern.

Holding a man whose warmth was only on loan, she surrendered to her exhaustion and sought refuge in sleep.

"It's beautiful. Absolutely beautiful."

They had emerged from the cavern into the clear, still, silent cold of Saturday morning. Just as they began the fifth day of their laborious trek, the sun broke through the surrounding peaks. It ignited diamond glitters on the vast snow slopes.

"Beautiful," A.J. agreed, stepping up into the saddle. He looked at her with those eyes that touched her like hands. He added, "But like most beautiful things, also treacherous."

She could still feel the tension pulling between them like a nettlesome mattress button, but a long sleep and the clearing up of the freak storm had restored her energy. The gorgeous, white, still life of snow in the high Rockies made her think of a line from one of her favorite poems: "The snow doesn't give a soft white damn whom it touches."

The vast, white slopes seemed to have the opposite effect on him. He seemed somber and reflective, almost subdued. She meant to ask him about his strange mood, but the hard twist of his mouth told her he wasn't feeling too chatty. Something was up, but she didn't know him well enough to probe.

"It's pretty," he told her. "But I can see right now the thaw has already begun. That means we have to watch for falling beds of snow on the rock ledges overhead. There's also going to be large icicles falling from overhanging cornices that form on the crests of the narrow ridges. They have to be avoided like falling spears."

He secured a safety line to her saddle horn.

"The reason we've got to make good time early on," he explained, "is that new snow slopes are usually hard in the early morning. By afternoon they'll be soft and maybe dangerous. The real problem up here is steep angles. Snow can't stay stable at an angle over thirty-eight degrees. A lot of the slopes up here are steeper than that."

She studied the pensive set of his strong jaw. "You seem to know an awful lot about snow. But of all the dangers we've faced before, you seem a lot more serious here—"

He cut her off. His mouth had the same grim set. "Let's ride," he said, ignoring the question in her tone. "Move slow and steady and keep your eyes to all sides."

She would ask him about the snow later, she decided. When they were warm and safe by the campfire. Now on the trail, she decided there could be too much of beauty. Both of them were quickly forced to don their sunglasses against the unrelenting snow glare. The mustangs had to be led into shade frequently to avoid snow blindness.

At first the numerous slopes were easy enough to ascend, especially with A.J.'s expertise to guide them. At the foot of each slope was a big crevasse. He led them directly up the expanses, carefully avoiding an oblique or horizontal track— such paths cut slopes across and increased danger of an avalanche.

Unfortunately the temperature rose quickly as the morning advanced. They were forced to a painstaking use of their ropes. He would advance upward first, secure the rope to a boulder or anchor pin, then wait for her to reach his position.

After a few hours she truly understood why the word *travel* came from *travail*. Her muscles ached, her feet were numb with cold, and each deep breath now included a little groan.

"Won't be too long now until Bridger's Summit," he assured her at one point. "How you doing?"

Instead of answering him, she produced her microrecorder from the pocket of her pullover. She thumbed it on and glanced down at the glittering series of slopes they had just traversed. She got her breath back before she spoke.

"The Chinese believe that before you can conquer a beast you must make it beautiful. I've made these slopes as beautiful, in my mind, as great sculptures. But I still haven't whipped them."

He smiled. "The Chinese, huh? Well, A. J. Clayburn says buck up. We're entering the home stretch now."

Travel, travail, buck up. Grimly she marshaled her last reserves of strength and will and followed him.

Make the beast beautiful and you will conquer it.

"Hazel," demanded Eric Rousseaux's irate telephone voice, "what is this nonsense my wife tells me? Something about Jacquelyn taking some fool-headed trip into the mountains. Do you realize there's a *blizzard* up in the peaks?"

"The blizzard I know about," Hazel replied pleasantly. "I know nothing, however, about any fool-headed trip. Your daughter and A. J. Clayburn are recreating Jake McCallum's historic ride across the Rockies for the sesquicentennial."

"That's another problem, Hazel. It's all over the media how some rodeo star and a young journalist are marooned together in a high-country storm. I'm not too happy to hear *my* daughter's name tossed into some kind of scandal."

Hazel had to bite back her first reply. Eric's horror of "scandal" evidently didn't include his numerous affairs with local bimbos and grass widows.

"Oh, Eric, you own newspapers. You know good and well it's always the silly season for journalists. It's harmless saloon gossip."

"Is it? The law takes a more serious view of a man's good name," Rousseaux hinted darkly.

Hazel laughed outright at the veiled threat, falling back on the patience her long years had taught her. By breeding and temperament she was an optimist. She believed that just about anything a person could dream was possible to achieve. Thus her own plan to save Mystery.

But she also realized there were natural-born dream killers lurking everywhere. She was talking to one right now. Had this man also managed to kill his daughter's dreams? When she looked into Jacquelyn's eyes, sometimes she wondered about it.

"Eric, I've been in touch with Bonnie Lofton, Jacquelyn's editor. You know that her husband, Ray, is the township constable. He's been monitoring the state-wide police band radio. The National Park Service has also been advised. Those two aren't lost—just temporarily cut off. Besides, it's for the sake of history. You should be proud of Jacquelyn."

"Look, Hazel," Eric said sarcastically, "we all know you long to return to the days before once-upon-a-time. Don't confuse senility with history."

"No, you look," Hazel said in her most pleasant, grandmotherly voice. "I've never been one to take the long way around the barn. Let's just say it plain—you don't care that much what happens to your daughter. You just don't want any inconvenience. Or to lock horns with me right now," she added meaningfully.

"Baloney, I—"

"I know why, Eric. It's because my grandfather wrote Mystery's present township charter."

"Woman, you are so full of—"

"And according to that charter," Hazel pressed on, "when it comes to land ownership, *families* are to get priority over any business not native to the area, namely ranching and farming. That makes it tough for you and your little Disneyland Wild West scheme, doesn't it?"

"Christ, you *are* losing it, Hazel. You need to do a reality check. Flush toilets are no longer a novelty. People today are into maximizing their profit potential. And that means a diverse portfolio."

"Save your energy, Eric. You'll need it to welcome your

daughter back home. You won't be subdividing any ranches here in Mystery. Oh, and you might not know this, but I have the majority votes on the town council.''

She was pleased by the choking sound she heard on the other side of the line.

"You won't get away with this, Hazel," he gasped.

"You," Hazel said sweetly just before she hung up, "are a bigger fool than God made you."

She wandered to the windows over the sink and pushed aside the waisted curtains to glance out toward the distant peaks. The storm presently obscured them in a soot-colored haze of clouds.

Knowing A. J. Clayburn, Hazel wasn't seriously worried about those two surviving the storm. She was far more concerned that a romantic spark might not arc between them. What she had told Eric about the township charter favoring families over businesses was correct.

That left only one obstacle to saving the character of Mystery: Hazel had to get some more families started, and quickly. As she held that last thought, her dreamy old eyes sought the distant peaks.

A smile touched Hazel McCallum's lips.

Thirteen

As long as she lived, Jacquelyn would never forget that last grueling stretch to Bridger's Summit and lonely Eagle Pass. A difficult ride in the best of weather, it was now made treacherous by huge volumes of rapidly melting snow and ice.

"The day's heating up too damn quick," A.J. fumed at one point as they spelled the horses and reset their saddles. He shuttled his glance toward the overhead ledges. "But the good thing is that snow avalanches never fall in unexpected places. We just have to stay focused on the danger spots, that's all."

Jacquelyn had become aware of a new edginess in him now that they faced snow hazards. It was hard for her to comprehend. This was the same man who had shrugged off a concussion. The same man who had faced down a charging bear. Not to mention man-killing horses in the rodeo ring. She had come to understand Hazel's faith in him. What she couldn't fathom was his sudden tightness when it came to snow. After all, he grew up in Montana. Snow was ubiquitous here.

Ahead of her he reined in. She let Roman Nose move up beside him.

"Do you see the cabin?" she inquired hopefully.

He shook his head, half his face in shadow under his hat. "Cabin's maybe twenty minutes ahead. Trouble is, we've got *that* to deal with."

He pointed with his chin, and she glanced above them on the narrow trail. As far as she could see, a rock ledge covered the route ahead of them. A rock ledge that was now precariously crowned by a melting snow cornice.

"You can see the places out ahead where it's already fallen," he added. "Look at that one pile—big as a house. That's solid-packed snow—weighs tons."

"Yes, but isn't it getting even more unstable while we stand here discussing it?" she said.

He gave her a grin. "By God, you're learning," he praised her. "But we'll need at least ten minutes to pass under the ledge. It's best to lead the horses, spread out at wide intervals. Tie this around your waist."

He handed her one end of his lariat, tying the other around his own waist.

"I'll go first," he explained. "Let me get to the end of the rope before you and Roman Nose start. Keep your eyes peeled overhead."

She had learned to trust his instincts. They had nearly cleared the dangerous overhead ledge. With each passing minute, more and more melt water splashed down on them. The back of her neck had begun to ache from staring overhead. Almost clear of trouble now, she let her gaze return to the trail ahead. Unfortunately the deadly fatigue that wore her down also decreased both her awareness and reaction time.

The moment a cracking, sliding noise began overhead, he

gave a mighty tug on her rope. Startled, she flew a few yards forward and landed in an ungainly heap on the ground.

A heartbeat later a car-size chunk of ice and snow exploded in fragments precisely where she had been walking seconds earlier.

It had only barely missed Roman Nose, too. Now she had to scramble to avoid being trampled by her sidestepping horse.

"Hurry on, dammit!" he urged her. "That loosed the rest so it's *all* coming down!"

But even as he spoke, the mass of the frozen overhang was cracking loose. Roman Nose leaped nimbly to safety. Jacquelyn, however, fell down trying to get traction in the snow.

A.J. gave up waiting. He pulled the rope taut and ran with it, literally dragging her the last twenty yards or so to clear the overhang.

Jacquelyn, facedown in the snow, heard a noise like the world exploding just behind her. Then she felt a shocking splash of ice fragments and ice-cold water wash over her.

"We're keeping you alive in spite of yourself," he chastised her mildly as he helped her up. "But I'm damned if we can keep you dry. You okay?"

She nodded. "Is the c-cabin close by, I hope?"

"We're only five minutes from Bridger's Summit. There's cordwood at the cabin if nobody used it. Have you dry and warm in two shakes."

Despite the chaos, he still had his bearings correct. Only a few minutes later they made their way around a big jumble of rocks. "There it is," he called out. "Snowed in, but looks fine from here."

She reined in beside him. The trail no longer seemed to be climbing now, and a flat clearing opened up like a fan before them. A small cabin of notched logs was protected by a man-made windbreak of rocks.

"I think we found the Ritz after all," she said, her teeth chattering in earnest now. "What's that out back? An outhouse?'' She motioned to a small, weather-tight shack now half-buried in snow.

''No, the outhouse is down the back slope, out of sight from here. What you're looking at is the springhouse. It used to cool food in the summer. See how it's built right over that little bubbling spring? That spring's one reason Jake bothered to haul wood up this high and build a cabin here.''

While they spoke they were moving closer, leading their horses now over the rocky, snow-slippery slope. A warm sun had created a multitude of little streamlets as snow melted. An old, rotten windlass beside the cabin creaked like rusty hinges in the wind.

''That lean-to off the cabin is for sheltering the horses,'' he explained. ''I'll take care of them while you get some dry clothes on.''

She stared at him. Things had sure changed in the last day or so. She was no longer the neophyte, worthy of ridicule. In fact, now he almost seemed concerned about her, and she wasn't sure she was ready for it. It made her more uncomfortable than his derision.

''No doorknob?'' she asked, staring doubtfully at the weather-warped, split-slab door.

''You think Jake had a hardware store nearby?'' he teased. ''See this leather latchstring? That's your 'knob.' If you're inside and you don't want the door opened from outside, you just pull it in when you enter. Not much problem with privacy up here, though.''

His gunmetal eyes met her gaze as he added, '''Course, it *was* a honeymoon cabin.''

''I'm here to absorb history, not relive it,'' she assured him, even though her cheeks burned at the remembrace of their hot kiss by the spring. She couldn't get the picture out of her mind. There was something about being fully clothed, and him being naked, that hit an erotic button inside her. She could never remember kissing Joe like that. Their time together had always been quick, clean and cool. He had wanted a woman to put on a pedestal, and when he'd found one, he could not allow her to fall from it. And so the freeze came. In the end he wanted Gina, he'd decided, who was slow, messy and hot. He could never allow Jacquelyn to be that way, and she had wondered if it was even inside her.

But now, thinking about A.J., she was sure she could be that way. Slow, messy and hot. Sure, it was in her all right. Because it scared the hell out of her.

"Better let me poke my nose in first," he suggested, looming behind her. "Sometimes critters take up residence inside."

He shouldered the door open, and a musty, closed-up smell wafted to their noses. She peered around his chest, impressed at the cabin's basically neat and orderly condition. Only a patina of undisturbed dust proved it wasn't occupied.

"All clear," he announced.

She saw a couple of cowhide-covered chairs and a solid deal table. An iron Franklin stove filled one corner, with a child's cradle now serving as a wood holder beside it. The stove was designed for both cooking and heating. Two walls held bracket lamps, and a brass cuspidor sat near one of the chairs.

"The hand pump and the metal sink were added in the 1890s," he explained. "Pump should still work. Most everything else is original."

He pointed to a bed of leather webbing along a side wall. "That thing is actually comfortable after you spread a sleeping bag on it."

Yes, she thought, but which *one* of us is going to be comfortable on it? And after yesterday, did the male-female formalities still apply? She didn't know. Right now she could only get some dry clothes on.

He quickly built up a fire in the stove.

"I'll take care of the horses," he said again, stepping back outside. "Then I think I'll do some fishing."

Before he shut the door he added, his tone laced with innuendo, "I'll leave the latchstring in."

Jacquelyn heated up a big pan of water on the stove, then stripped off her wet clothing. Nervously watching the door, she gave herself a quick but thorough bath and washed her hair. Feeling like a new woman, she pulled on her last pair of clean jeans and a soft cotton shirt.

When A.J. returned, his hair was wet and slicked back.

"Took a skinny-dip in the brook," he boasted. "Colder than polar bear poop."

He slacked into one of the cowhide chairs, weary. She watched him stretch out those long legs and cross them at the ankles. For a moment their eyes met and held. Both of them glanced away, self-conscious.

"I set a trotline up," he told her. "There'll be at least two fat bass or trout on it by suppertime. Look in that cabinet behind you."

She did. Airtight metal containers were labeled Flour, Sugar, Salt, Coffee, and Baking Soda.

"Any bugs in that flour?" he demanded. "I brought it up fresh my last trip here."

"Eeech. Bugs?" She twisted off the lid to inspect it. "Looks fine."

"Good. Woman, you are in for one legendary treat. The Clayburn men make the best biscuits in the West. My biscuits are so light you have to hold 'em down."

She smiled at his boasting tone. No Southern macho man worth his gun rack ever boasted about his cooking skills. In Montana, however, cowboys even got into fistfights defending their cherished recipes for stew or biscuits or chokecherry cobbler.

"Fresh fish and hot biscuits," she marveled. "A veritable feast after the fare of the past few days. All we need is some wine."

"Let not your heart be troubled," he assured her, a gleam in his eye. "Look behind the canisters."

She slid them aside and spotted an unopened bottle of Old Taylor bourbon.

"Not exactly wine," he conceded, "but Jake hated wine. Said it was nothing but vinegar sneaking up on old age. Colonel Taylor was a war buddy of his. So Jake allowed no other spirits but Old Taylor in his house. But it'll do to wash our teeth."

Normally Jacquelyn avoided alcohol, disheartened by her mother's unhealthy dependence on the stuff. But marooned on top of the world like this, and plagued as she was by this growing yearning—maybe a "spot of the giant killer," as her mother called it, might be in order.

By now the cabin was cheerfully warm. She felt so exhausted she couldn't stifle her yawns.

"Take a nap," he suggested. He spread his sleeping bag open on the leather webbing. "When you wake up, I'll fix our supper."

"Wait a minute," she challenged, unable to take it anymore. "Where's the tough guy who refused to help me with my tent? Gave me a lecture how he was nobody's slave? Now you tuck me in and fix my supper?"

He grinned. "Yeah, I know what you're thinking. Still flattering yourself that I mean to expand my harem. But that woman I refused to help a few days ago hadn't *earned* my servitude. The woman I'm with right now saved my butt on Devil's Slope. Us Clayburns don't forget a debt like that. I owe you a good meal."

So it was just a point of honor, she thought, feeling oddly disappointed. Did that disappointment mean she *wanted* him to scheme and seduce her? Had she lost her mind?

She gazed at the temptingly comfortable-looking bed.

"Well, maybe just a little catnap," she said, giving in.

For all her awkward feelings, sleep claimed her only moments after she lay down. But her rest was haunted by disturbing, confusing dream sequences.

She saw vivid images of Jake and Libbie in the flush of their youth. Laughing in the brittle morning sunshine; holding each other in the evening twilight on the summit; a pair intertwined as one to face the cold, harsh, workaday world far below them.

Only, in an eyeblink, the faces would change. Jake and Libbie became Joe and Gina, their eyes mocking Jacquelyn—who always stood off to one side of the dream scenes, watching everyone else's happiness like a rented video. *See how it's done, ice princess?* Joe's eyes taunted her.

When she woke up, the cabin windows were pitch-black with night. Both kerosene bracket lamps glowed brightly. A delicious aroma of hot food filled the room.

"There you are," he greeted her, standing near the stove. "I was about to hold a mirror in front of your mouth, see if you were still alive."

"Why didn't you wake me?" she asked sleepily.

"Hazel says you never pick up a happy baby." He gave her a strange, curious glance. "You know anything about babies?"

She flushed a little as she stood up and straightened her clothing. "Not a thing."

"I hear they're easy to get." He smiled deviously with a mouthful of strong white teeth.

She looked at him. "I'm surprised someone like you doesn't have a stableful of those right now, too."

"Thinking about getting me some." He looked down at what he was cooking.

She suddenly felt very warm. Too warm. "Well, I wouldn't know about all that," she offered, uneasy. "I'm more the…the filly type rather than the brood mare type, if you catch my drift there, cowboy."

"Ah, you underestimate yourself."

She opened her mouth to tell him he'd got it all wrong.

But then the effort seemed too much. She wasn't going to make him into a yuppie, and he wasn't going to make her into Annie Oakley, so there was no point in bothering.

"You sure you're okay? You frowned a lot in your sleep. I watched you," he added.

"I'm fine," she said, perhaps a bit too defensively. "And maybe you shouldn't be watching me."

"Takes too much effort not to." He glanced at her again with those dark gray eyes like a thunderhead. "Only a fool makes an effort to avoid seeing what's pretty."

She was rattled, unsure where he was going with all this. "I know that's probably a compliment," she admitted.

"Not really," he dismissed, rattling pans and seasoning fish. "Taking credit for a pretty face is like bragging when you're dealt an ace. Hell, that rhymed! Why'n't you quote it?"

"Maybe I will," she said, again trying to hide the stab of disappointment at his words.

There it was again, she told herself, feeling more hurt and baffled than angry. The recurring theme: looks don't equal character. A pretty face and a good figure were little more than an empty shell if they were hollow inside.

And the irony of it all. Here she was on a trek that somehow seemed to be trying to teach her character, as if her looks had ever helped her. As if anyone had ever bothered to know what she was like inside. She only knew that she wasn't the one who needed character. She wasn't shallow. It was others who were. Others who saw only surfaces, only ice. Not the heat that bubbled below, not the hidden human yearnings. Not the fiery heart and warm spirit.

"You're frowning again," he informed her. He pulled the chairs closer to the table. "Come eat. Part of your problem is just plain old hunger."

"I'm really not too—"

"You'll eat," he insisted, "and there's the end. I'm damned if I slaved over this hot stove so you can nibble on granola bars. East Coast rabbit food! No wonder you can't keep up a head of steam.''

Despite her foul mood she laughed at his motherly fussing. Part of it was put on, but part of it was genuine.

"Okay," she said, surrendering. "I'll eat. But can't a girl get a drink around here to whet her appetite?"

He raised an eyebrow like a melodramatic villain. She watched him use a case knife to turn the fish, sizzling in a black iron skillet atop the stove.

"A drink? Ladies drink free in this saloon. You'll find a few glasses in the cabinet. Pour me a jolt, too."

She found two barrel glasses and wiped the dust out of them with her shirttail, then she cracked the seal on the bourbon bottle and poured a couple fingers of the shimmering amber liquid into each glass. She handed one to him.

"To Jake and Libbie," he proposed.

She smiled. The perfect irony. "To Jake and Libbie." She clinked her glass to his.

The bourbon burned in a straight line to her stomach, smooth but strong.

"Oh," she breathed, her eyes filming with tears. "That's…volatile stuff, isn't it? I'd better watch it."

"'Nuther?"

He tempted her by lifting the bottle.

"Maybe."

He laughed. "Yeah, I see how you're 'watching it.'"

She took down her second drink like an old pro, even smacking her lips. "It grows on you, doesn't it?"

"Like a lot of other things," he answered, his words heavy with meaning.

"S'matter, cowboy?" she demanded with a smile. "'Fraid you'll get hurt by Miss Manners?"

He looked at her with a crafty glint in his eyes. "I'll be damned, you little firecracker." He eyed her glass, then filled it up again. "We better feed you while your…appetite is good."

"You do that, rodeo boy," she flung at him, meeting his eyes until he actually turned away, flustered. Now it was her turn to laugh on the offensive.

"I'm whacking the cork on you, lady. No more hooch until after supper."

"Well, you're no fun," she dismissed.

"Oh, yes I am," he told her almost in a whisper. "More fun than those dreams that make you frown. So much fun that liquor ain't needed. Now you *eat*."

Fourteen

Hot food filled her, and the giddy light-headedness deserted her. A dulling sense of lethargy also followed as the sudden alcohol high ebbed. The cabin grew small again. Every movement between them seemed exaggerated and almost ominous. Jacquelyn felt the raw sexual tension between her and A.J. lurking like a coiled beast in the shadows.

"Guess you can tell I don't drink much," she confessed as she pushed her blue-enameled plate away.

"Yeah, I noticed. Good thing you don't, too. You'd be an easy mark."

She gave him a weary smile. "I believe the saying is 'She's a cheap drunk.'"

"It's all one."

"Delicious supper," she mentioned, quick to change the subject. "Thanks."

She became aware of a faint sound like tiny claws scratching at the windows.

"It's snowing again!" she exclaimed, her voice climbing

an octave with sudden apprehension. "I can hear it pelting the windows!"

"Don't worry, nervous Nellie." He sipped his powerful cowboy coffee from a battered metal cup and watched her across the table from caged eyes. "It's just big flakes—a drifting snow, not heavy pack. This ain't no Die-up."

This ain't no Die-up. She'd heard lots of Montana natives say that when discussing weather. The "Great Die-up" of 1886 was the state's worst winter on record. Snow piled up past the eaves of houses, and entire herds were smothered to death in the cattle-rich Judith Basin. The animals couldn't be fed, and the starving cattle even resorted to eating tar paper from the walls of shacks.

"Speaking of snow," she said, watching his angular, cleanly handsome face in the burnished lamplight, "why does it bother you so much, A.J.? The way you seem to know so much about it—you're like a soldier who's studied the enemy he fears and respects."

He'd heard the question. She could tell that from the way he looked at her, a little irritated. At first he said nothing. She had already noticed something about the way A. J. Clayburn engaged in so-called conversation. It was actually more like taking a deposition, where he always elicited information, but seldom gave any.

This time, however, he surprised her with an answer, albeit a confusing one at first.

"Angle of repose," he told her cryptically.

"Pardon me?"

"I said angle of repose. That's why I respect the snow so much. It's an engineering term. Refers to the exact angle where the weight of a given substance overcomes gravity. Like when a solid ridge of snow becomes a moving avalanche."

"There you go again," she said, impressed. "Are you an armchair disaster expert?"

"Nope. Not knowing anything about angle of repose is

what killed my parents when I was eight years old. They didn't know a thirty-eight-degree angle means snow can give at any moment. That ignorance killed them.''

He spoke matter-of-factly, simply answering her question. But she suddenly felt heat behind her eyes as she recalled the look in his eyes back on those slopes. Mystery explained.

"I saw it happen," he added. "I was skiing on a nearby slope. We all dug for hours, but over two hundred tons of snow slid on top them. They were pulled out way too late.''

Heavy silence lingered between them.

Finally she whispered, "I guess I found an old wound. I'm sorry.''

"Hell, I was just a kid, anyway. Nothing I could do about it. But you know, it haunts you all your life when something like that happens. You run it over and over in your head, wondering if you could have done *some*thing to save them.''

The distant expression in his eyes mirrored his words. "They were both just…'' He clearly struggled to control both his voice and his emotions. "They were both just…just gone in a heartbeat. One moment I was laughing at them while they clowned around. The next, they were buried in hundreds of feet of snow. It kinda left me…'' His words faded again.

"Left you what?'' she pressed with a whisper.

He shook his head as if trying to clear it of his turbulent thoughts.

"I don't know,'' he admitted. "It just kinda left me afraid of…forever. That everything I cared about would be taken away from me *forever*.'' He paused for a long moment. "God, it's an awful word. *Forever*.''

As he gave voice to these painful memories, the only sign of his inner tension was his tightly doubled fists on the table in front of him.

Her heart swelling, she placed a hand on each fist.

"You were too little to help them,'' she reminded him. "But you saved *me* today when that snow ledge collapsed.

From their tragedy came your vigilance that saved me. Your parents would be proud of you.''

"Saving you was just a moment of weakness," he said from a deadpan, and she slugged his arm.

"Far as them being proud of me," he resumed, "it sounds crazy, but my becoming a rodeo champ was partly meant to do that, even though they're gone. You know…somehow, in my mind, that accomplishment makes up at least a little for my helplessness as a kid.''

It didn't sound at all crazy to her. Her own secret dream, to someday become a nationally respected feature writer, was also a form of compensation. Yes, her own parents were still alive. But they, too, had left her with a powerful sense of inadequacy—of ''helplessness,'' to use his word.

Only now did a note of bitterness creep into his tone.

"Trouble with being a rodeo champ—you're only as good as your next ride. And with my knee busted up so bad in that last throw, I might not *get* a next ride. That World Cup ain't like a Superbowl ring you get to wear for life. It has to be won all over each season.''

"So what if you do have to retire from the rodeo circuit?'' she countered earnestly. "It has to happen sometime. Nobody can take back your accomplishments. And anyhow, I can't see you growing paunchy and lazy in middle age.''

"If it was just for my own sake, I'd hack it fine. Every pilot gets grounded someday. But…ahh, I feel like I had a present. And now they're taking it back, y'know?''

She was still holding his clenched fists. Her heart responded completely to the plaintive sense of longing in his voice. She knew full well what it meant to want something unattainable. To have presents given, then asked for back. In the same futile way that he had sought to impress his dead parents, she sought a love and a sense of belonging that appeared forever beyond her emotionally limited grasp.

For a long moment their eyes met across the table. Her pulse quickened with some unspoken expectation.

He stood up, and she tensed, not sure what was about to happen or what she meant to do about it. But he only crossed to the stove, banged open the rusted iron door and tossed in a stove-length of wood.

However, he stopped behind her chair on his way back. His strong hands began kneading her sore shoulders and back.

At the very first contact she almost drew away. But some other part of herself told her this was what she needed right now. Maybe even what he needed.

"Mmm." She finally surrendered, feeling her muscles grow heavy with relaxation.

"You sober now?" he said close to her ear, his voice low and husky.

"Yes."

"Good. I guess that has to mean," he told her as his hands slid around to the top button of her shirt, "that I have your willing consent to do *this?*"

He undid the top two buttons and slid his hands inside her shirt.

Her instincts were to stop him, but then she wondered why she should. She hadn't been with a man since Joe, and he was ancient history. True, she wanted more than a quickie with a beefed-up rodeo star, but if that was all that was offered her, what was keeping her cold and alone tonight? It sure wasn't propriety. That had gone by the wayside days ago. Love figured in the whole thing, but love had passed her by once, and she was hardened to it now. It couldn't hurt her again. She wouldn't let it.

She felt him unfastening her bra. Closing her eyes, she reveled in the warm weight of his hands gliding around front to cup her breasts. The first electric contact teased her nipples erect, and she moaned.

"Permission granted?" he demanded.

Her breath quickened. She nodded.

"And how 'bout *this?*" he asked her, bending down to cover her neck with little kisses like erotic tickles.

She trembled as if she were cold. But she was not cold. Definitely not cold.

"And *this?*" His mouth met hers.

She responded to his probing kiss with more heat than she thought inside her. Only now—overcome by want and tension—did she realize the true depth of the desire that had been building between them for days now.

Even now, as she matched the passion of his kisses with her own, a cautious voice warned her that *this,* too, was only a form of "compensation." A. J. Clayburn was her social and temperamental opposite. Later she might pay dearly for this moment of escape.

But the desire his mouth fired in her overcame all caution. Need was making her mindless, and right now mindless was what she wanted to be.

He pulled his mouth back from hers, only with an effort.

"Now I'm done asking permission," he informed her, sliding his strong arms behind her back and knees. "Let's get to it. In my sight, it's been long overdue."

Effortlessly he lifted her from the chair and carried her to the bed. He finished removing her shirt and bra. Moaning from her pent-up desire, she barely recalled him peeling off her jeans and panties.

He dropped to his knees beside the bed and hotly mouthed her torso while he took his own clothes off. His lips traced a moist path from her nipples to the taut ivory concave of her stomach.

The heat of his kiss moved lower, and she felt his strong hands on her inner thighs, parting them. When his greedy mouth tasted the wet heat of her sex, she felt melting waves of pleasure build and wash over her, each surge more intense than the one before it. Only now, as a powerful climax surprised her, did she realize how much desire for this man she had been suppressing and denying.

She cried out, subjugated by a deep sexual release.

Immediately she craved more pleasure, and when he stood to join her on the bed, she knew she would have more as she got a stunning view of his nudity in the golden lamplight.

His legs were long and muscular, his hips lean, with a stomach flat and hard as a board. Flat, hard pectorals met shoulders corded with muscle. Foreplay had left him hot and erect. A pulse at his temple throbbed with each heartbeat.

"So you really are a flesh-and-blood woman," he whispered to her.

She felt strange emotion clog her throat. With a hunger she didn't know she possessed, she tilted her lips and kissed him, proving her mortality and need.

Gasping, she took his hard length inside her. Above her he groaned. So he was mortal, too.

Consumed, she locked him between her thighs and ran her hands down his hard-muscled buttocks. He moved against her, cupping her bottom with his callused palms, driving deeper and deeper into her.

Orgasm racked her body twice before he gave his final thrust. Then she closed her eyes, savoring the sweet violence of his release, savoring her name upon his lips. But the lull didn't last long. To her dismay she realized A. J. Clayburn was a strong and greedy man. His climax only seemed to drive him wild for more, like the scratch that only caused more itching.

Around dawn they took their peace. She drifted off to sleep, her naked, exhausted limbs intertwined with his.

For this one sweet night, and for this one ice princess, the cowboy had met his match.

Fifteen

———

"**D**ammit, Larry," Eric Rousseaux snapped into the telephone, "you just don't get it, do you? If we can leverage enough votes on the town council, it doesn't *matter* what Hazel McCallum's charter says. It doesn't matter a frog's fat ass. If the U.S. Constitution can be amended, so can Mystery's township charter."

Eric was doing dumbbell curls while he spoke to his business associate. As usual he'd left his shirt off to reveal his well-honed physique. Never mind that he was in his den where no one could appreciate it.

He frowned into the phone. "No, don't change the subject by asking about Jacquelyn. You watch the news. You know damn well they haven't returned yet, but that's not what I'm talking about here. And I don't want to hear you whine about Hazel. I'm not a man who likes to lose. Get those votes or you're fired."

He was about to speak again when Stephanie suddenly appeared in the doorway, a bottle of cognac in her right hand.

His wife visited him in his den about as often as Halley's Comet passed overhead.

Great—she's drunk and there's going to be a scene, Eric thought. But making scenes was not her usual way. If anything, Stephanie's self-control was downright scary.

"Larry," he said brusquely, "we'll wrap this up later."

He set the phone on his desk, still watching Stephanie with a wary, expectant look. Oddly, though, her eyes seemed clear, and her little ironic smile was not in evidence. Ten at night, yet evidently she was still sober.

"Was that really Larry?" she asked him in her throaty voice. "Or Linda or Lucy or Lana or—"

"Very funny. Larry and I were just discussing details about Mountain View. What do you need?"

"What do I *need?*" Her tone mocked his words, but she was not being combative. "Don't get me started, dear heart, because you won't like the list. But I didn't come up here to talk about my needs. I realize that topic is of no interest to you. I'm just curious, Eric. Our daughter is up in that pass, maybe fighting for her life. Do you care at all?"

The unexpected question left his face etched with annoyance. "What the hell's this all about?" he demanded.

"You heard me. Here you are, cooking up shady business deals while your only child may be fighting for her life. It leaves me curious, is all. Your indifference toward me is perhaps understandable. I'm partly to blame. But what did Jacquelyn ever do to you that you could be so indifferent to her fate?"

"I am not indifferent, just busy! I love our daughter as much as you do...but what am I supposed to do? I called Hazel. You heard what the state police commander told me. A full-blown rescue effort can only be initiated after sure confirmation of an emergency. We don't know that Jacquelyn is in any trouble. Frankly, she could be snug in a motel with A. J. Clayburn, for all we know."

Stephanie stepped into the den. A strength appeared on her face that hadn't been there before.

"You know she's not that kind of woman," she said. "And I know you know it, because you have more experience with that kind of woman than any man I've ever met."

"Go to the kitchen," Eric said, his voice becoming more caustic. "Go anywhere in this whole damn house, but don't get in my face about that subject again."

Stephanie raised the cognac bottle so he could see the contents.

"Normally," she explained, pointing with one finger, "by this time of night the level would be down to about here. But I did something different tonight. I decided to stay sober and think about how I've been *blessed* with Jacquelyn. And you know what, *my* life is full of blessing. My life with you is not."

"What's that supposed to mean?" Eric crossed the den and took her arm, shaking her.

"What that means is I'm leaving you, Eric. When Jacquelyn returns—pray God that she does—I'm getting a lawyer and leaving you."

"You're crazy. This Clayburn fellow—I've been told that young man could hike straight through hell and come out without a heat blister. When she's back, you'll regret everything you're saying tonight."

"Even if she does come down safe from the mountains," Stephanie pressed, "I will be leaving, Eric. I can't save the world—hell I can't even save my own daughter right now—but I can save myself."

"Save yourself? What the hell from?"

"*You*, Eric. You and me. Together we are poison, and we managed to poison our only child's life as well. Neither one of us has thought of anyone but ourselves. Are you even aware, for example, that Jacquelyn's been miserable for months now? That her heart was broken to bits back in At-

lanta when Joe Colbert threw her over for that Gina Galla-
tin?''

Eric shrugged. ''Ahh, young love…it's combat of the
heart, you know that. There are always casualties.''

''Yes, but when you're badly wounded, some first aid
would be nice. But neither one of us was there for Jacquelyn.
We *never* are. She's alone, and no amount of your money
can right the wrong we've done to her. Not even *all* your
money.''

The truth of her words pierced Eric's heart like a needle.
''I can't believe you're doing this.''

Stephanie's voice cracked with cynicism. ''You know
what, Eric? I can't believe you care.''

Jacquelyn was the first one awake on Sunday morning,
momentarily disoriented in the dawn stillness of the cabin.

One wall lamp had burned itself dry of kerosene, the other
was guttering like a candle in the wind. She saw her clothes
forming a puddle with A.J.'s beside the bed. The sight of her
pink cotton panties dangling off one of his scuffed boots
shocked her eyes wide open.

Oh, God in Heaven, what had she done?

Even though she had not gotten drunk last night, she felt
the panicky regret that follows a wild bender—except that
she couldn't even blame her reckless decision on alcohol.
A.J. hadn't left her that option.

She chastised herself for her abandon, but her rebellious
body sent little signals that *it* felt quite satisfied, thank you,
by last night's events. Her lips were swollen from his rough
kiss. And when she carefully sat up in bed, an intimate sore-
ness made her recall the…exuberance of their passion last
night—and well into the morning.

When her bare feet hit the raw lumber floor, reality slapped
her fully awake.

She gazed at the handsome man slumbering peacefully beside her, his face unlined in sleep. Last night they could not

get enough of each other. Indeed, the urgency of their coupling seemed to suggest they resented being two separate bodies. But now, with this new day, all that seemed gone. Like a fist when you open your hand.

Her wanton passion had now turned into astute apprehension. She didn't know how to face him again. What tone should she use? Intimate, or just friendly? Caring or impartial? There were too many choices and not enough time.

Sick inside, she wondered how he would act when he awoke. What would be his assumptions? He could not have expected the hot little siren she'd become last night—would he expect more of the same in the future, perhaps another taken-for-granted perk of his star status?

He muttered something in his sleep, and his voice galvanized her into action.

She quickly dressed and ran a brush through her hair. Then she poked the fire to life and soon had a pot of coffee perking. As the aroma deepened and wafted throughout the cabin, it seemed to prod him awake.

"Remember," his sleepy voice called from under the covers, "it ain't strong enough unless you can—"

"Cut a plug off it," she finished for him. "I know, cowboy. I'm a quick study."

"Well, if you've got all that under control," he suggested, his deep voice lazy and thick, "why'n't you hop back in bed?"

His tone made it clear he wasn't suggesting extra sleep.

"Maybe," she proposed in a neutral voice, avoiding his eye, "we should talk about plans for returning? I really do need to get back."

It sounded lame and cold even to her, but it was easier to make obvious excuses than to figure out the turmoil of her feelings right now.

"Sure," he said after a long pause. "We can talk about going back."

If a voice could frown, his just did. Clearly he could not

believe this was the same woman who had left fingernail scratches stinging his back.

Here I am again, she thought desperately. Freezing him out because I can't find the words or courage that I need.

He pulled on his jeans and stepped outside for a few moments. When he returned, he poured himself a cup of coffee.

"It's warming up quick outside," he told her, looking her flat in the eyes. "The snow that's exposed to direct sun will melt right away. But that's only the first snowmelt. Most snow actually falls in shadow pockets the sun can't reach too well. It takes longer to melt—usually days."

He frowned and spat his coffee into the sink. "Quick study, huh?" He poured the rest of his cup out.

"Anyhow," he continued, staring at her as if he were trying very hard to see something that wasn't there, "we've only got two realistic options. From here it's only a one-camp ride down into Mystery Valley. So we can move quick before the first snowmelt gathers enough force to choke off the fords—"

"Or...?"

He stared directly into her eyes, letting her see the challenge revealed in his tone.

"Or we wait a week or so up here for both melts. Maybe have that honeymoon after all."

She felt the panic rise in her chest. "I couldn't," she spoke up too quickly, realizing too late he was only being ironic.

"Whoa, Your Highness, don't get all spooky on me. Neither could I. I've got a business to run down in the valley. So we'll pull out right away this morning. But I'll warn you right now, we'll have to make good time. I've seen heavy rainstorms flood Thompson's Creek. That happens, it closes the trail just below the pass. Snowmelt could do the same, so we have to move fast."

She nodded, relief surging into her. They had to move fast now, and that meant less time for talking, less time for analyzing, less time to manufacture goodbyes.

She started gathering her things together, but something he'd just said prompted her to ask, "You mentioned a business you run in the valley? But Hazel told me you were helping a friend who operates a rodeo school?"

"I do, but that's just a favor." His eyes dismissed her.

She asked no more questions. Remorse was already setting in as she realized how *wrong* the morning had turned out. And it was her fault. The ice princess had returned, and she didn't know how to make her go away.

They ate a hasty breakfast of leftover biscuits spread with honey. Neither one of them seemed to know where to look while eating, and her own feeble attempts at conversation died on her lips. He wasn't interested, and why *should* he be? Last night she had literally climbed all over him; now she was scared and keeping him at arm's length. From his perspective, she must seem like a Jekyll and Hyde of the heart.

After eating, they quickly rigged the horses for the homeward journey. At one point, still tormented, she almost got up her courage to break through the ice floe.

"A.J.?"

She watched him raise a stirrup out of his way and tighten the girth. Resentment was clear in the strong set of his features.

"Yeah?" he said, eyes never leaving his task.

Experience was a cruel master, and she feared what might happen if she gave up the safety of her own controlled isolation. So often, when she'd tried to open up to Joe, she'd only been crushed for her efforts. For her the best defense had become more defense.

"Nothing," she finally replied. "I'm ready to ride."

"Long as you got what you came for," he said ambiguously as he swung into the saddle.

The downhill riding, once below the snow slopes, was far easier for their return trip. Yet, if anything, Jacquelyn found the descent into Mystery Valley even more awkward than their ascent to Eagle Pass.

Nonetheless, there wasn't as much animosity simmering between them now, at least not so openly. Their conversations were stilted and at times peppered with sarcastic innuendos, true. But at least they got beyond a mere trading of insults.

"You asked me about my family," he reminded her during their first stop to spell the horses. "And all about Jake's. So what about yours? I mean besides the fact that your old man is trying to pave our cattle ranges. What's it like growing up pretty and privileged?"

She took no offense at the "paved ranges" comment. On that score, at least, she felt the way he and the rest of the locals did.

She delayed answering for a few moments, breathing deeply of the clean, cool air. Narrow and winding Eagle Pass lay well above them now. She watched the horses stretch their necks toward a stream to drink, their muscles sharply defined in the coppery sunlight.

"I guess some people have called me pretty," she told him, mustering a smile. "As for the 'privileged' part—my father loves to remind me there's no such thing as a free lunch. For your information, he doesn't give me a dollar of my money. I waitressed for four years in college to pay my living expenses. And I've worked since I graduated."

"You sure stay busy," he conceded, adding reluctantly, "and you do top-shelf work, too. Pardon me saying so, but I wish your pa cared as much about Mystery as you seem to."

"He's got different priorities," she said, treading carefully.

He definitely seemed to be in a listening mood. So she tried to make him truly understand how difficult it was growing up the daughter of Eric Rousseaux, hypercritical perfectionist. How she had to be perfect all the time or face his devastating disapproval. But she couldn't find the right words to fully convey what it was like, as a child, to die a little inside each day. Just as her mother had done.

"I guess," he commented as they mounted their horses, "you can be an orphan in more ways than one. Tell me something else."

She looked directly at him now, but he chose to feign interest in something out ahead of them on the trail.

"Maybe I will," she replied. "What do you want to know?"

"Seems to me I remember past summers where some tall, tennis-player type used to fly out here to hang all over you. Haven't heard about him being around this summer."

The irony of that one made her flinch. "Not this one nor the next," she assured him. As they rode on she told him a few succinct details about becoming the odd-woman-out for Joe and Gina.

"We got a word out here for people like them," he commented. "They're secondhand, both of them. It's not the number of lovers you've had that makes you secondhand. It's whether or not you treat 'em cheap."

She thought she detected a tone of accusation in his last remark. Did "people like them" include her?

She stared at him and thought hard about what she should say next.

He preempted her, calling her attention to all the runoff streamlets gathering force all around them.

"Best hurry," he snapped, seeming glad to change the subject. "The lower we go, the more meltwater we face."

Clearly, their intimacy the night before had changed his manner toward her. While not exactly courtly or even solicitous, he was civil and considerate toward her now. A vast improvement over his former surliness and indifference.

But the changes were not just in his manner. In truth she saw him in a different light from last Monday in Hazel's parlor.

Though she hadn't intended to sleep with him, it was not

merely lust that motivated her. For one thing, letting that angry bear actually claw him when he could have killed it had proved to her he had a tender side. And his confessions about his parents still clutched at her heart. He clearly had been left with a deep-rooted fear of loss he'd never been able to shake. A guy like that would be way more comfortable going from woman to woman than pledging his troth to one and risking all.

As they made their way down the slopes, she began to wonder about what was to become of them. She wondered and then froze inside.

Last night was probably going to turn out to be just like all the rest of his sexual escapades. Short and meaningless. She would bump into him in town in a few months or a year, and he would look at her like a stranger.

He would tip his hat to her, then walk away.

And she would watch him go, forcing herself to remain cold inside. Keeping the permafrost intact.

And then maybe, instead of thinking of the night she clawed his back as if grabbing back her hope, she would go to the liquor store and order up a case of cognac.

Sixteen

"**I** started out in high school as a rodeo clown out in Red Lodge," A.J. explained in answer to Jacquelyn's persistent queries about his story. "'Cept I learned quick there ain't much clowning about it. Their main job is to distract killer bulls and outlaw broncs from attacking a downed rider. Figured long as I had the danger, I might as well get the glory, too. So I started competing."

Now and then afternoon sunlight glinted off his nickel-studded belt. They rode back among the trees now, following McCallum's Trace through a stand of birch and scrubby jack pine.

"I've ridden hurricane decks from El Paso to Calgary," he added, using a favorite cowboy term for bucking broncos. "The rodeo at Red Lodge is still my favorite."

Trouble clouded his eyes, and he knew he was thinking about his last injury. She wished she could say something to reassure him. But in truth her own glum mood precluded such sympathy.

It had finally sunk through to her that she had completely misjudged this man. In fact, he was just the kind of man she would want, if she honestly consulted the ideals in her heart. He was strong, decent, capable of deep passion and rock-solid commitment. He was everything she suspected Joe was not.

With a man like A. J. Clayburn to judge other men by, she suddenly found a well of pity inside her for Gina. Her friend would get backhanded by Joe's shallowness one day, just as Jacquelyn had.

She swallowed the thick lump of unshed tears in her throat. If the trip had proved anything to her, it was that she was well rid of Joe. It also had managed to dangle something much more tempting in front of her, but the brass ring was too far for her reach. She and A. J. Clayburn were like day and night. He probably did have that harem of fans waiting for him back in Mystery, and she would do well to keep it in mind. There was no point in getting attached and watch her dreams tumble like an avalanche. Their lovemaking along McCallum's Trace was like her being atop a bucking bronc: momentous to her, another day's ride to him.

With every passing hour of their descent into Mystery Valley, she grew more and more quiet. With every hill her heart tightened with the dread of rejection.

He seemed distant, as well. As if he were still trying to figure out, as was she, what the hell happened between them up in that cabin.

"Heads-up, news hawk!" he called out late in the afternoon. "Don't you want to mention *that* into your tape recorder?"

He pointed across a rocky marsh, and her attention followed the end of his finger. The scant remains of a settler's cabin were heaped in a little clearing. But he was pointing out the hand-painted sign nailed to a pine tree out front. The whitewash letters were still faintly readable: TRESPASSERS

WILL BE SHOT AT AND IF MISSED WILL BE PROS-
ECUTED!!!

"Old Dad Gillycuddy used to pan for color up here," he
informed her. "Never found gold, but he became one of
Montana's most famous hermits. He referred to any settle-
ment bigger than fifty people as 'syphillization.'"

"Thanks for speaking loudly," she said, showing him her
recorder. "I got all that you said. This Dad sounds like a real
friendly guy."

"Oh, 'bout like you," he suggested, starting his horse forward again. "Took what he wanted on his own terms."

"What's that supposed to mean?" she asked, not sure if
she wanted to know.

"Which part confused you, college girl?" he called back.
"It was a short sentence spoke in simple English. Hell, I'm
just a dumb cowboy. How could I be confusing?"

Whatever it meant, his implied insult only worsened her
emotional isolation. By the time they'd pitched their final
camp of the grueling expedition, her defensive cocoon was
woven tight. On the surface, little had changed. But in the
secret locket of her heart, there was only room for survival
skills—and not the mountain kind.

"Out West," Jake had written in one of his letters home,
"you're just a face with a name. Nobody really cares about
your history." That was one reason why Jacquelyn had
looked forward to escaping to Mystery this summer. But even
way out in Montana, you brought your problems with you
like bad habits.

A.J.'s voice broke into her thoughts, ending a long silence
beside their crackling fire.

"We're back home now…damn mosquitoes," he mumbled, slapping his nape.

She herself had been bitten several times in the past few
minutes, but she was too despondent to notice the welts.

He took a look at her face that was no doubt red with fresh

bites. "Damn things are in swarming season. I'll be right back."

He returned in about fifteen minutes carrying his coffee cup, now filled with plump berries.

"These'll keep the skeeters off if you rub the juice on your skin," he explained. "Here…you have to squeeze it like this."

He took her left hand and extended her arm, rolling the sleeve up.

"Just pinch the berry 'tween your thumb and finger, and keep the fat end next to your skin. Like that. Then just massage it in."

She stared at him as he worked the clear, sticky juice into her skin. His touch ignited a crackle of sexual response within her. She said nothing to him, she made no move, but her insides were slowly being consumed by flame.

Forcing herself, she spoke simply to end the awkward pause. Awkward pauses could lead to trouble….

"I guess this surprise storm made for big news around the state, huh? I can't wait to see a newspaper."

"Couldn't've been a total surprise," he mentioned absently. "I saw it coming last Monday night."

He seemed to immediately realize his mistake. Even in the subdued firelight, he watched her stunned expression.

"Monday night?" She repeated his own words like an astounded Inquisitor. "You knew *before we left?*"

"I saw the potential," he amended hastily.

Sheer exasperation made her speechless.

Finally she demanded, "Did you plant the snake in my sleeping bag, too?"

He gave her his direct stare.

"Would you rate my performance as a lover so low," he asked her quietly, "that I need to use tricks to get laid?"

She felt herself grow cold in the darkness. Is that all it was for you, she wondered—getting laid? But instead she said,

"I have plenty of complaints about you, A. J. Clayburn. But that is not one of them."

"'Preciate *that* much, at least," he nearly snarled, his words cutting her like a dragoon's blade.

"Look," she forced herself to say, each word an agony, "we've been through a lot here. At least at parting, couldn't we try to be friends?"

He stared at her, the expression in his gunmetal eyes frosting over. "Friends, huh? You mean, like maybe me giving you my phone number just in case you need a handyman—or maybe just someone to ride one night? God, woman, you are cold."

Giving her a derisive glance, he stood and retrieved his bedroll.

His wounding talk had paralyzed her. She hadn't expected the anger, the rejection quite so soon. But more so, she hadn't expected his arrows to hone right in on her weakest, most vulnerable point.

She watched him wrestle with his bedroll. Almost as if she was acting on another's bravado, another's will, she swallowed her fear and went to him.

"I'm not cold," she whispered, touching his thick arm where the muscle wrapped like bands of steel.

He stopped what he was doing, straightened and looked her right in the eyes. "Not cold?" he taunted. "Prove it."

Trembling she placed her hands on either side of his face. She pulled him down to her, ignored the distrust in his gaze and kissed him, her tongue licking deep, hot and messy.

He groaned. Wrapping his arm around her waist, he lifted her to him, pulling her off the ground. His own tongue penetrated her with a hard, wanting kiss, and she knew instantly she had to have him, if just for one more night.

"I'm gonna regret this," he mumbled as he scooped his bedroll off the ground and threw it inside the fly of her tent.

"I don't want you to," she whispered before his mouth silenced her with another deep kiss.

He pulled her into the tent, then ripped at her shirt. A small pink button popped off and rolled away. Neither of them seemed to care. If the night was growing chilly, Jacquelyn didn't notice in the heat of their lovemaking. Before she could even fathom what they were doing, she was naked, lying on top of him while he cupped her buttocks and kissed her with all the passion in his cowboy soul.

Unable to wait, she let him roll her to her back and enter her. His large hard body moving against her softness took the breath from her lungs. After only a few moments her hungry pleasure came hard, with him quickly following. But when they collapsed into the sleeping bags, she knew they had only taken the edge off their appetites. They had one last night. And there would be no more.

With sunrise on Monday morning, Jacquelyn dismally rolled up the tent and broke camp. The silence betweem them was leaden. She cursed the fact they now had only a few hours of mostly easy riding remaining. Soon they would descend the final slope to the eastern edge of Mystery Valley. Soon they would part. And then, after that…she didn't want to think about what would happen then.

"Let's go," he said, bringing over Roman Nose fully tacked up. He gave her a long, moody stare before handing her the reins and swinging up onto his mount.

She followed him, desperate to change the course of events. Before dawn, as they lay in each other's arms exhausted and sated, she'd asked him if she was going to see him again. All she got was the uneasy laugh, then the questions.

What? Are you gonna give up your city life and come rough it with me here in Montana? Another laugh.

You with your fancy Beemer, and you're gonna ride around with me in my old pickup?

Are you willing to spend the next fifty years correctin' my

English while I tell you what an uppity woman you are?
More laughter. Cold derisive laughter.

Her answers to all the questions were always yes, but she
never spoke them. She kept her yesses silent.

Now hurt and confused, she only wondered when he
would be ready to hear her answers. But that time could only
come when he stopped pushing her away. He was guilty of
all he'd accused her of. With his hard heart, more frozen than
her own from the pain of that avalanche so long ago, she
wondered if the time would ever come that he would offer
to be scared and tell a woman he needed her.

So for now she kept her thoughts on the trail and pushed
away the tears that threatened to overflow at the slightest
suggestion.

Luck had been with them at quick-flowing Thompson's
Creek. Although snowmelt had already swollen the creek
over its banks, they were just able to cross on a gravel-bar
ford A.J. knew about. They were making fabulous time.

She wished one of them would fall and break an arm.

Well before noon they rounded a huge rock abutment. As
if an image had just been flashed on a giant screen, Mystery
Valley suddenly appeared before them in all its verdant, sun-
shimmering glory.

"Home at last," she exclaimed quietly. It was practically
her only comment since they'd risen.

Even A.J., who'd had to have seen this panoramic vista
often, seemed humbled into silence.

Far below them, freshly rain-washed meadows gleamed in
the sunshine. The town of Mystery was a tiny cluster of toy
Monopoly buildings near the center of the valley. Hazel's
huge Lazy M spread was clearly visible west of town.

"Let's get to it, then," he murmured darkly, pushing his
mount onward.

She followed, hardly able to believe they'd been gone just
a few days and not a lifetime. She had been through so much.
Now she had to sort it out, for right now none of it made

much sense. Except that she had fulfilled Hazel's strange request. She was changed forever.

The ice princess was back with a vengeance. A frozen surface deflected what could not be safely absorbed—at least until, she reminded herself blackly, it finally shatters from the stress.

Early Monday afternoon they arrived back in town. But a final surprise awaited them on the lower slopes just beyond the town limits. A herd of matching shiny pickup trucks, each pulling horse trailers awaited them in the parking lot where they'd left A.J.'s vehicle. Amazed at the strange gathering, she couldn't help but speculate out loud.

"Is there a horse show going on?' she asked when she dismounted.

An off-road Blazer, with the shield of the Colfax County Constable on the door, lumbered up to them. A silver-haired lawman wearing timber boots and a wide-brimmed hat waved a friendly hand at them. She recognized Bonnie Lofton's husband, Ray.

"Damn, A.J.!'' he shouted to them. "You're officially being rescued! Congratulations! We got every rider from Clayburn Ranch out looking for you, and here I'm the one who finds you in the parking lot. I'm a local hero now, son. Sure am!''

A.J. laughed.

Jacquelyn looked at the horse trailers all painted the same snow-white with the Clayburn logo painted on the sides as if to mimick a brand.

"Clayburn Ranch?'' she questioned. "But I thought you just helped out Cas Davis at his ranch—''

He cut her off. "My old rodeo buddy Cas Davis use to sponsor me back in the early days when the corporate boys hadn't noticed my riding yet. So I help him out on weekends. But I run a horse-breeding farm on our homestead with my two younger brothers. You ever heard of the annual Bucking Horse Sale in Miles City?''

She nodded. Even tourists knew it was a huge exhibition and auction for rodeo-stock contractors. A lucrative business in Montana.

''We sell a majority of the horses each year.'' There was quiet pride in his voice. ''Our own breeds, just for rodeo and show riding. The Clayburn brand is on more world-champion rodeo horses than any other.''

She stared at him, absorbing this next facet of his character. So the granite-jawed cowboy was also a successful businessman.

Looking around at the fifteen matching pickups and trailers, she almost laughed at A.J.'s old truck, sitting in the back of the parking lot. ''And you really do just drive that old pickup because you like it,'' she commented.

He gave a curt nod. ''So is that important after all?''

She didn't know how the silence damned her, but she was too caught up in her own jumble of thoughts to turn his around.

A.J. turned to Ray, giving him a puzzle-headed grin. ''So nobody's working the ranch? They're all up in the mountains looking for me? I'll fire every one of 'em when they return. They know better'n that.''

Ray just smiled and handed him yesterday's edition of the area's only daily newspaper, the *Helena Sentinel*. She walked Roman Nose over so she, too, could read the triple-deck headline above the fold on page one:

RODEO CHAMP, JOURNALIST, LOST IN MOUNTAIN STORM

She knew she had to have turned as pale as the snowy peaks above them.

"Bonnie left it out of the *Gazette*," he told her, as if offering consolation. "Looks like you two went out to get the news and *became* it."

A.J.'s glance searched out her evasive eyes. "Looks that way. Too bad nothing happened. Not one damn thing."

"Hell, A.J.," Ray scoffed, playing up a bit to the rodeo champ. "None of us lawmen thought you were in any trouble. And the cowboys? Aww, man! They're *still* joking about how you and—"

Ray caught himself just in time. He looked at Jacquelyn and cleared his throat, embarrassed.

Even A.J. winced a little. "Yeah, Ray," he said, "I catch your drift. 'Nuff said."

Jacquelyn caught the drift, too. The ache inside her swelled. It was clear she was just going to be another filly in the A. J. Clayburn paddock. He was the way he was, and her ice princess heart wasn't warm enough to change him no matter what they'd been through together.

There was now no point in lingering over the goodbyes. She handed Roman Nose's reins to A.J. and turned to Ray. "Think you could give me a ride back to Mystery?"

Ray looked at A.J., hesitant and unsure. "Not a problem. I know your mom's going to be glad to see you, Jacquelyn." Sensing he wasn't needed, he unbuckled her packs off her pony and took them to his vehicle.

She turned to A.J. "Please tell Hazel I'll call her tomorrow about the article."

"You're the boss," he said with cryptic sarcasm, rapidly stripping his horse of its rigging.

She paused. The knot in her throat threatened to suffocate her. All she could think of was getting away, being alone to lick her wounds in peace. "I guess that's about it, then. Shall I pay your fee myself, or has Hazel taken care of it? Or was this trip gratis in light of the entertainment value?"

He folded his arms across his chest and stared at her with eyes gone glacial. "Consider it gratis," he clipped, his handsome features set like stone. "A. J. Clayburn never charges a stud fee. Not even to rich women who can afford it."

Taking both horses by their bridles, he turned his back on her and headed toward the trailer and old pickup, leaving her devastated.

"It was sweet of you to come here and let me know how it went, A.J. At my age I love getting out, but I hate driving," Hazel said, breaking a long silence in her best harmless-old-lady voice.

A.J., sitting across from her in the McCallum Victorian parlor, even distracted as he was, didn't buy her act.

"Only time you ever bring up your age," he reminded her, "is when you're up to some trick."

Hazel raised her eyebrows. "Are you angry at me, A.J.?"

He gave her a snort. "So what if I am? Never stopped you before. Besides, Hazel McCallum's tricks—whatever they are—usually turn out good for Mystery."

She smiled. "There's the spirit! It's like eating your spinach, right?"

"Never touch it," he snapped. "Rabbit food."

She laughed outright while he lapsed back into the brooding silence that had characterized him during the visit. Whatever happened up in those mountains, Hazel thought, had clearly been *important* to him. That was the first hopeful step.

"So tell me…you think Jacquelyn got a good story?" she asked, her tone merely conversational. Getting information out of a typical cowboy was a tricky business. They were not known for "emoting." Mainly Hazel hoped to gauge his manner, then draw her own inferences.

"If she didn't get a good story," he retorted, his tone heavy with contempt, "to hell with her! I'm damned if I ever take her up there again."

Oh, yes, Hazel gloated, this is looking quite promising.

He fidgeted in the chair, then stretched out his legs and crossed his arms over his chest. His stare was baleful.

"These women that grow up rich," he blurted out, "think they're God's gift to men."

"They can be snooty," she agreed with diplomatic neutrality—thus egging him on.

"Just so *damned* silky satin," he added scornfully. "Expect you to spit when they say hawk."

"They can be prideful," she agreed.

"Prideful? Hell, *I'm* prideful. She's—"

He caught himself. "Some of these rich women go beyond prideful. Just too damn precious to be owned, yet everything they see is their toy."

The pent-up resentment in his tone left Hazel positively gleeful. This had gone even further than she'd hoped! She decided to roll the dice.

"A.J., correct me if I'm wrong. What you're trying not to say is that you're in love with Jacquelyn Rousseaux?"

For a long moment Hazel feared even she—A.J.'s lifelong friend—may have gone too far. But finally he answered her.

"She's the highest card I've ever been dealt," he confessed in a miserable tone. A moment later, however, he seemed to recover his fortitude and determination. The jaw was granite again.

"But it's no use," he charged on. "There ain't no way in hell two people like me and her could have a future."

"No," Hazel chimed in thoughtfully, "I don't suppose there is."

"And even when she found out about Clayburn Ranch, she still didn't care. I couldn't make enough money to please her."

"I heard money doesn't mean a whole lot to her, but, of course, you would know better than I would on that score. You're the one who spent all those nights up on the mountain with her. I guess you got to know her pretty well, didn't you?"

He didn't answer. His eyes filled with a sad, stormy expression that looked almost like guilt.

"And besides," Hazel added pointedly, "Jacquelyn Rousseaux is certainly not your kind of woman. She's the type that's for keeps. You couldn't possibly have her, A.J., because you'd have to marry her, and you don't really need a woman around. Too much bother, I think you've always said."

He seemed tormented by her words. He struggled for a moment, but whatever hope was inside him he seemed to dash. "Well, anyhow," he said, still trying to convince himself, "the trip's over now, and there's an end on it. I won't have to bear *her* high-hatting ways ever again."

Stand by for the blast, Hazel warned herself.

"Now, A.J.," she told him in a placating voice, "there is one more little…situation that has come up."

He looked over at her, his gray-blue eyes wary. "Hazel, nothing you get involved with is *little*. What 'situation' do you mean?"

"You *are* handsome when you get mad."

"Then I must be damn good-looking right now."

Hazel grinned wickedly.

"Hazel, you sly witch, quit stalling me. *What* situation?"

"Well, while you and Jacquelyn were gone," she replied, "there was a township meeting. We crushed old Eric Rousseaux and his plans for Mystery with the bottom of our heel, I don't mind telling you that, but the price was high. After the meeting, several people wanted me to curry their favors, if you know what I'm getting at."

"Yeah? About what?"

"Well…brace yourself," she warned him, still stalling. "Just look at it as your duty."

"*What,* dangit all?"

Hazel opened her mouth to explain. Then suddenly she chickened out.

A.J. stared at her. "It's that bad, huh, that you're scared to tell me?"

"Frankly, yes," Hazel replied. "And telling you will be the easy part. Lord help me, tomorrow I'll have to tell Jacquelyn."

Seventeen

Jacquelyn went straight home and mumbled a barely civil hello to her relieved parents. Postponing their torrent of questions, she promptly fled to the guest house and locked the door. She cried herself into a deep, and mercilessly dreamless, sleep.

That long rest did wonders for her resolve, if not her happiness. She woke up on Tuesday morning determined not to let A. J. Clayburn torment her mind and heart.

As for all the "saloon gossip" as Hazel liked to call it—so what? *Let* A. J. Clayburn turn her into his latest bunkhouse boast. What did she care what a bunch of crude hicks in chaps thought about her?

She had foolishly surrendered in a moment of exhaustion and weakness. Blame the seductive pull of the cowboy's tragic story about his parents. As a matter of fact—if he had deliberately misled her regarding the weather, who's to say he didn't deliberately exploit his own parents' death? All to "get laid" as he so romantically put it.

The low, despicable monster, she thought, condemning him without benefit of evidence or trial.

She steeled herself for a difficult and busy day. First she had to check in with Bonnie at the *Gazette* office and see what work had piled up in the past week while she'd been gone. Then, as Hazel had requested in a message, Jacquelyn was going to stop by Hazel's later in the afternoon to discuss the trip.

Jacquelyn showered, luxuriating in the plentiful hot water after the rigors of the trail. She selected a cool sheath dress from her closet. It felt good to finally be out of blue jeans.

She sat down before the triple-mirror vanity to put on a pair of black-onyx earrings. In the mirror she saw her mother suddenly appear in her doorway.

"So how was it?" Stephanie demanded.

"How was what?"

"Look at you, all wide-eyed and innocent! I mean, so how was it being up there all alone with A. J. Clayburn and his sexy bedroom eyes? Hubba-hubba?"

Jacquelyn flushed, and her eyes cut away from her mother's reflection. "You're up early," she commented just to change the subject.

"No hangover to nurse, that's why. I haven't touched a drop since Saturday. It's amazing how early you can get up when you aren't passed out drunk."

Despite her own miserable mood, her mother's words coaxed a smile onto Jacquelyn's face. "Good for you," she said encouragingly.

"Yeah, but listen, you. There's also a downside when your old mom stops juicing. Now you gotta talk to me now and then. You know what? While you were gone, I realized we don't talk enough."

Jacquelyn smiled at her mother in the mirror. The Rousseaux home certainly had not turned into a fairy-tale existence while she was gone. But clearly something was different.

"Matter of fact," Stephanie added hesitantly, "I've decided to leave your father. I guess I'm getting so clearheaded sober, you might decide you prefer me drunk."

Jacquelyn let the news sink in. She wished she could feel bad about her parents' divorce, but deep down she knew it was the healthiest move her mother had ever taken. "I'll let you know if I prefer you drunk, Mom," she promised. "But don't count on it."

She turned away from the mirror to look directly at her mother. "Did something happen while I was gone?" she asked, curiosity getting the better of her.

"Sure. Absence makes the heart grow fonder and all that. You know what, honey? I was scared."

Stephanie turned to leave. But something pensive and distracted must have appeared in Jacquelyn's face that made her instead step into the bedroom. She crossed to Jacquelyn's side and placed a hand on her shoulder.

"Yesterday, when you came home, it was clear you were terribly upset. I was on the verge, just now, of telling you not to make so big a deal out of...whatever happened up there in the mountains. But you know what?"

"What?" Jacquelyn whispered.

"Maybe our mistake—mine and yours, I mean—is that we need to do just the *opposite*."

"I don't follow."

"I mean—maybe we're wrong to always blow things off. To simply bury things out of sight. Maybe we need to make them *more* important, not less."

Stephanie gave her a quick, embarrassed hug and left.

Jacquelyn sat there motionless, pondering all that her mother had said, but the memory of the last night in the mountains contradicted her. Then Jacquelyn had thrown away all her armor. She had begged A.J. not to think her cold, not to think her an ice princess any longer. She'd let herself go, done messy things, just so he would forever know she wasn't the woman he thought she was.

But in the morning the fire had grown cold again—*his* fire. She was nothing to him but another notch on his bunk. He wasn't capable of loving her, of even feeling the power of the moment as she did, because he would have to get attached, and that he'd vowed never to do.

At least not to a woman like her.

The tears she'd thought she'd managed to get under control came flooding back. Her eyes stinging, she put her head down on her dressing table and sobbed.

When Jacquelyn arrived at the *Mystery Gazette* office, Bonnie was at work in the darkroom and the red safelight over the door was turned on.

Jacquelyn had only a few messages on her desk, none of them timely or important. Her In basket contained a few new story assignments. Mostly just short fillers and news items for "The County Roundup." Stuff she could bang out in no time. She sat down at her desk and began to sketch out a working outline for her story about riding McCallum's Trace.

Coming back to the office, she realized, was like a dose of therapy for her emotion-charged psyche. She welcomed the familiar, reassuring pressure of a deadline as well as the demands inherent in writing a compelling feature article. No "writer's block" for her, thank you. Because then she'd have to face these awful questions and insecurities that were sure now to forever plague her in idle moments—like the baffling question of A. J. Clayburn and what, if anything, might have happened to them if things had been different.

The safelight over the darkroom door winked out. Bonnie stepped into the office carrying a stack of freshly printed and dried black-and-white photos.

"*There's* our star reporter! Back from riding the high lonesome. Kiddo, we were worried about you."

"So was I," Jacquelyn admitted. "A few times, anyway."

"Oh, goody! That means we'll get an exciting story out of it. I've already had a request from the *Cheyenne Ledger* to run the story. They've picked up your entire series on Jake, off the wire. The editor there told me you're his favorite Western feature writer. Of course, I didn't bother to tell him you're a Southern belle. He assumed you're a native cowgirl.''

Jacquelyn felt a smile tugging at her lips. ''Believe me, this one is going to be the best installment yet. After all that work and danger, I can now finally appreciate that old headline.''

She nodded toward the wall behind Bonnie. A yellowed copy of the inaugural issue of the *Gazette* was framed in glass and rosewood. The lead headline combined straight news with a sort of advertisement: Men Needed for McCallum Trail Drive—Orphans Preferred.

''So how did you get along with A. J. Clayburn?'' Bonnie asked her, though much more discreetly than Jacquelyn's mother had.

''Actually, not so well,'' Jacquelyn answered truthfully. After all, only a few hours had been spent in bed with him. As blissful as those interludes had been she had to admit it was a case of sleeping with the enemy. Most of the time they clashed like Greeks and Turks.

Bonnie seemed puzzled by this report; indeed, she seemed to expect a different answer altogether. But she said nothing about it.

''You must be scrambling to get ready for the Frontier Days Ball this weekend,'' Bonnie said.

It was Jacquelyn's turn to look puzzled.

''Scrambling? Why? I'm only covering it for the paper.''

Now understanding gleamed in Bonnie's eyes.

''Ooops,'' she said. ''I take it you haven't talked to Hazel yet?''

Jacquelyn felt her stomach sink. ''No, not since I came back. Why?''

''I think,'' Bonnie said with judicious caution, ''that maybe I'd better let Hazel tell you that.''

"Bonnie!"

"Sorry, hon."

"Has she 'volunteered' me for something else?" Jacquelyn demanded.

"You know Hazel," Bonnie dismissed. "She's what the old-timers used to call a 'notional' woman."

Right, Jacquelyn thought. But no more notions involving A. J. Clayburn. Jacquelyn figured she'd paid her dues on that score.

"Well, if you're going to play coy," Jacquelyn carped, "I guess I'll have to wait until I talk to Hazel this afternoon."

Bonnie headed toward the layout table, sorting through her photos.

"I'm not playing coy," she assured Jacquelyn. "I'm just plain chicken."

"So it's *that* bad?"

Bonnie shook her head. "That'll be for you to decide. But just to prepare you—based on what you've said about A.J.? I don't think you're going to like Hazel's plan one bit."

"Jacquelyn, you look wonderful," Hazel praised the younger woman as she led her into the parlor. "If your lovely skin suffered any, my old eyes can't see it."

"Thank you," Jacquelyn said as she settled into a wing chair. Her mind was preoccupied with the things Bonnie told her. But Jacquelyn knew Hazel well enough to understand she did things by her own schedule. And the woman expected everyone else to accommodate her. So Jacquelyn had no choice but to let Hazel control the conversation.

"Although," Hazel qualified, studying her closer, "it appears your…allergies are back. Your eyes look a little red."

Jacquelyn offered a rueful smile at Hazel's skeptical emphasis on the word *allergies*. "Can't fool you, huh?"

"Not for one minute," Hazel replied complacently. "Thank you, Donna," she added when her housekeeper brought them coffee and pastries, setting them on a stone-inlaid table between the two women.

"So tell me about McCallum's Trace," Hazel urged her. "First of all, was I right? Didn't it change you?"

Jacquelyn hadn't expected that question, even though she'd thought so much about it. So she opted to duck the issue.

"Surely you already asked A.J. about the trip."

Hazel tapped the excess sugar off a Russian tea cake, shaking her silvered head in amusement at Jacquelyn's stonewalling.

"A.J. is many things, but he's not a yakker. Men like him—they don't talk much more than they have to."

Jacquelyn felt her face heat up. "Not around you, maybe. He respects you, Hazel. In fact, he seems to think the sun wouldn't rise without your approval. But when it comes to finding fault, to criticizing and harping and picking away at…well, at others, believe me, he likes to talk plenty."

She swore the old woman gave her some kind of "atta girl" look. Jacquelyn felt as wrangled as a wild horse.

"I *wish* he didn't talk any more than he had to," she forged on, working up a head of resentful steam. "Conceited? My God, from bucking horse champ to god of the galaxy! And the man has no concept of civility. He's…he's a bully, that's what. Arrogant, insufferable—"

Jacquelyn suddenly realized she was practically raving, and Hazel was smiling with cherubic joy about it. Was the old girl dotty, after all?

"'Arrogant,'" Hazel repeated, nodding. "'Insufferable,' yes, I don't doubt. And you're in love with him, aren't you?"

Jacquelyn's wide eyes went even wider with astonishment, and she almost dropped her cup. She was so flabbergasted, she just stared at Hazel with almost childlike defenselessness.

"Hazel," Jacquelyn began to protest. But before she could fashion a huffy defense, she burst into unexpected tears.

"My goodness, honey, you *are* in a state," Hazel said, rising and crossing to her chair.

Jacquelyn was past all defenses now. When Hazel squeezed onto the wide chair beside her and took her in her arms, the younger woman wept copiously.

"God, I am so stupid," Jacquelyn said bitterly between sobs. "Letting myself get involved with a man so utterly different from me."

"Sweetheart, what's that got to do with anything? Doesn't the yin complete the yang or whatever?"

Jacquelyn couldn't help a brief smile at Hazel's analogy.

"Well, anyhow," she resolved, sniffing into her handkerchief, "there's absolutely no law that requires me to interact with him. Ever again."

"Interact?" Hazel repeated, bemused. "Is that what you younger girls call it now?"

Jacquelyn blushed when she realized which "it" Hazel meant.

"But, dear," Hazel added, "I ought to tell you—a little something has come up in your absence."

Jacquelyn nodded, wiping her eyes. "I know. Bonnie said you have something to tell me."

"Yes, well, sometimes duty calls, doesn't it?"

"Duty?" Jacquelyn repeated skeptically.

"Why, of course, dear. Civic duty, I mean. You see, while you two were up in the mountains, there was a final township meeting. Mainly, we had to tie up loose ends to kill your father's project—please give him my sincere condolences, will you? But we also needed to fit out our sesquicentennial celebration for this coming Saturday. That's the day of the Frontier Days Ball, if you remember."

Jacquelyn nodded, already knowing all this.

"Someone suggested," Hazel resumed, "that it would be wonderful to have one of our own local young couples portray Jake and Libbie. They could arrive by fringed surrey, wearing authentic period clothing, to officially open the whole celebration.''

Jacquelyn felt the blood drain from her face. '''Someone' suggested it, Hazel?''

The old dame spread her arms in a gesture meant to suggest her helplessness. ''Oh, who knows how the proposal got started, but my Lord, was the suggestion popular! It was voted on and passed unanimously.''

''Voted on?'' Jacquelyn repeated. ''But that's…how can a vote replace my permission? Have I been drafted?''

Hazel clapped her hands, delighted with that. ''Yes, that's it! You've been drafted to serve your community. Now come along, dear, I have to show you your gown. I already know it will fit you because I talked to your mother to confirm your size.''

Jacquelyn made a token effort to resist when Hazel tugged her up from her chair and led her into an adjoining bedroom.

''It was actually owned by Libbie,'' Hazel explained, leading Jacquelyn toward an emerald-green silk ball gown on a wooden dress rack. ''She paid a local dressmaker to copy it from a European fashion doll. Libbie designed the bustle herself. I think her side-lacing silk boots will fit you, too.''

''Hazel, it's beautiful,'' Jacquelyn said, staring at the rich, foreign clothing. ''But it's impossible. I went along with your idea of the trip into the mountains with A.J. Now I've *spent* my time in hell. He doesn't want anything to do with me, and I don't want anything to do with him. Now I must put my foot down. Please 'draft' someone else.''

''Honey,'' Hazel soothed, ''it's not just me. It's popular demand. You can't disappoint the entire community, that's not your way. Besides, think what fun it will be to play old-time dress up! As for A.J.—if you really can't abide the fellow's presence, buck up. You hardly need to spend much time alone with him. Just a quick ride from my place to the town square.''

''Oh, Hazel,'' Jacquelyn said, somewhat exasperated as

she felt herself crumbling again before this woman's steam-roller will. "Does A.J. already know about this?"

"Told him yesterday. He's going to do it."

"Of course. He'd burn down a church if *you* told him to. But don't fib to me, Hazel. Tell me, how did he take it?"

"Well," Hazel replied after a preparatory sigh, "quite honestly? Let's just say I'm now convinced that nothing on earth could ever make A. J. Clayburn hit a woman."

"See?" Jacquelyn challenged, her insides tightening with hurt. "He doesn't want to, either. It's a bad idea, Hazel. I...I realy just don't think I could get through it." That was an understatement, at best. To look at A.J. again after all she'd confessed to him, all she'd revealed to him, all she'd *done* to him, was more that her spirit could endure.

"Hmm," Hazel replied mysteriously, looking at her visitor with a speculative eye. "Of course, you do have that short hair. So we'll be sure to include a bonnet."

"I give up!" Jacquelyn exclaimed. "I never had a choice, anyway."

"No," Hazel agreed sweetly. "Because your only choice is to say no. And that's not choosing, that's being a coward. And Jacquelyn Rousseaux is no coward. She's a mixed-up young woman in love, and she's going to confront that fact come hell or high water."

Eighteen

By 8:00 p.m. on Tuesday, most of downtown Mystery had rolled up the sidewalks. But Bonnie Lofton was still hard at work in the *Gazette* office.

Bonnie was laying out the special sesquicentennial issue, which would be in the corner coin-ops and rural paperboxes by early Friday afternoon. She had left a "double truck"—two facing pages in the middle of the paper—blank for Jacquelyn's feature. With Hazel's and Jacquelyn's input, Bonnie had already selected most of the historic photos and documents that would support Jacquelyn's article.

The usual Wednesday deadline had been pushed back one day so that Jacquelyn had more time to edit and polish her story. Bonnie had heard a first draft over the phone. It made her feel the excited expectation she always experienced before the release of one of Jacquelyn's major assignments. The girl's talent made the job *fun* again. Suddenly, a little sixteen-page weekly from a remote Western valley was turning heads in far-off places.

It was peaceful in the office, the heavy tick-tock of the old case clock's mechanism lulling her. So Bonnie actually started in fright when the phone on her desk abruptly burred.

Still pasting down a headline with one hand, Bonnie speared the phone with the other.

"*Mystery Gazette,* Bonnie Lofton speaking. May I help you?"

"Howdy, Bonnie, it's A. J. Clayburn. I called your house, and Ray told me you were still working. What, you night watchman now, too?"

Bonnie laughed. "No, I'm not due for promotion yet, A.J. What a surprise to hear from you! What's up, cowboy? Got some news for us?"

"Maybe I do, at that. Tell me, Bonnie. Has Jacquelyn finished her story about our trip?"

"Well, an early draft."

"You read it?"

"She read it to me. It's wonderful, A.J. Weaves historical details with a gripping account of the trip you two made."

"But did she write anything about how she saved my life on Devil's Slope?"

"Saved your *life?*" Bonnie repeated. "Why, no. She described a harrowing avalanche, but nothing... Well, I'll be darned! She saved your life, A.J.? Really?"

"As sure as God made Moses," A.J. confessed, sounding a little bitter about the fact. "Not just that...while doing it, she executed one of those fancy steeplechase-style jumps like she was born to the saddle."

"It's just like her," Bonnie mused, "to be too modest to mention it in her own article. I guess she's too professional to toot her own horn."

"Can *we* toot it for her?" he suggested.

Bonnie grinned. "Sure we can. We'll team up for a little sidebar story next to Jacquelyn's. You describe it, I'll bang it out. It'll carry both our bylines. Fair enough?"

"Fine by me," A.J. agreed. "People'll think I'm literate."

"We'll even keep it a surprise from her," Bonnie added,

warming to the scheme. She picked up a pencil. "Now tell me more about this heroic rescue, A.J."

Hazel finished tying the muslin bonnet under Jacquelyn's chin, then stepped back to admire this newly transformed nineteenth-century beauty.

"Ta-*dumm!* Ladies and buckaroos, I present the Southern belle of the Western ball! Jacquelyn, you look absolutely beautiful. Or at least you will when you stop frowning."

Jacquelyn—bustled, bonneted, and gloved—stood looking at her reflection in a tall cheval glass. It was eerie, she thought, how precisely Libbie's emerald gown fitted her. As if this night were meant to be.

"You're fortunate, dear," Hazel reminded her as she pinned a beautiful silver and garnet brooch onto Jacquelyn's bodice. "Hoop skirts were not yet all the rage when Mystery was founded. Otherwise, we'd have to rig you up wider than the seat of the surrey. A.J. would have to trot beside the team."

Then dig out some hoops, thought Jacquelyn resentfully. Her stomach fluttered with dread at the thought of facing A.J. again.

It had been four days since she reluctantly agreed to Hazel's latest meddling scheme. And with each day that passed, Jacquelyn felt more like a condemned woman whose last appeal had been rejected.

"Dear," Hazel chided her gently, "you needn't look as if someone just kicked your dog. You've got to get in a celebration mood. My goodness, you act as if you're afraid of A.J. Honey, it's true he's all man. But he's *only* a man. The entire sex is eternally doomed to defeat when they clash with the feminine will. And they know it, too."

"A.J. doesn't know it," Jacquelyn insisted. "And if he knew it once, he's long since forgotten."

"That so?" Hazel said, stepping back for one final look. "Then perhaps you'd better be a real woman and remind him of his place."

At these last words Jacquelyn felt a little prickle of shock. The "grandmotherly" tone left Hazel's voice when she spoke them. My God, she just gave me a direct order, Jacquelyn realized. Is she going to slap my face, too, and tell me to "nerve up"?

Hazel's sweet manner returned instantly. She glanced at her watch. "I'll have to leave in a few minutes, dear. I'm the grand marshal, so it won't do to show up late. A.J. will be here shortly. The surrey is hitched and ready in the side yard. *Do* put a fine face on all this, won't you? This means so much to the entire town, not just to old fuddy-duddy me."

"I'll need a blindfold and earplugs to complete my outfit...without them, I'll just have to do my best," Jacquelyn quipped.

Hazel dismissed her with a wave. "Oh, fudge! I know what you're talking about—your morbid, self-pitying belief that you are incapable of true *caring*. We all have that at times, but, honey, what is wrong with you and what doctor told you so? You little fool! Stop worrying about that strutting peacock back in Georgia and his ignorant opinions. Women who 'don't care' don't risk their lives as you did to save A.J."

Jacquelyn's green eyes went even wider with surprise. "So A.J. told you about that?"

"Told *me?* My lands, girl, where have you been grazing? He told the world!"

Lately, Jacquelyn had been so gloomy and preoccupied with this night, that she hadn't even bothered to read yesterday's *Mystery Gazette*.

Hazel crossed to an oak highboy and scooped up the newspaper lying there. She handed it to Jacquelyn.

"Turn to your story," Hazel told her.

Jacquelyn did. Immediately her lips parted in surprise. A sidebar box ran alongside the copy for her feature. It carried its own headline: Rodeo Champ Says Heroic Reporter Deserves Medal.

And the greatest shock of all—A.J. shared the byline with Bonnie.

The story was brief and factual. A.J. even admitted to his stupidity when he stood up in his stirrups at the wrong moment. The article described Jacquelyn's actions as "quick horseback thinking, competent, gutsy and graceful."

"I…I didn't know," Jacquelyn stammered. Here she believed she was the butt of lewd jokes, when in truth she was being feted as a heroine.

"Well, now you do," Hazel remarked as she aimed for the door to the parlor. "So why don't you adjust your attitude accordingly? Now I have to head into town, dear. Donna will let you know when A.J. arrives. Remember—" Hazel wagged a finger at her "—frown all you must on the trip into town. But once that surrey rounds the courthouse building, I want ear-to-ear smiles on *both* your young faces, you understand? The town square will be rightly lit and very crowded. So remember you are Libbie and Jake and you are *in love.*"

"I'll try," Jacquelyn promised, wanting very much to roll her eyes.

"Not try," Hazel corrected her. "You'll do it. You survived McCallum's Trace. This little ride with A.J. won't whip you."

Jacquelyn mustered a smile. "You're something, Hazel. For God, for country, for Mystery—right?"

"You don't even realize," Hazel confirmed before she shut the door, "just how true that is."

The evening sky was deep purple with twilight when A.J. arrived to escort his "bride" to the Frontier Days Ball. Preoccupied as she was, Jacquelyn had forgotten that A.J., too, would be in period dress.

Her first glimpse of the handsome frontiersman startled her. He looked spiffy and well set up in a gray summer-weight suit with a frilled white shirt and octagon tie. His usual Stetson had been replaced by a broad black plainsman's hat. A gold watch chain trailed from the fob pocket of his vest.

"You look very well," Jacquelyn said with stiff formality while A.J. escorted her, arm in arm, to the surrey.

"Thanks," A.J. replied brusquely, not bothering to meet her eye. "You're easy to look at, too."

He handed her up into the carefully maintained fringed surrey. It was, in fact, an original McCallum vehicle from the early days of Mystery Valley. The handcrafted beauty had been stored in the wagon shed until a few of Hazel's hired hands recently rolled it out for service. Now there was fresh blacking on the dashboard and a new whip in the socket. A handsome, seventeen-hand blood bay gelding stood in the traces.

Jacquelyn cringed inside each time she peeked over at A.J.'s frosty, tight-lipped face. My God, he wants to be here even less than I do, she realized.

He lit the running lamp suspended from a pole near the driver's spot. Then he unwrapped the reins from the brake handle and swung up onto the seat. He gave the reins a quick tug.

"Gee up, Rip!" he called out to the gelding. "Hep! Hep!"

The surrey sprang forward. As it turned through the stone gateposts of the Lazy M, she finally mustered her courage to speak.

"A.J., Hazel just showed me the article you and Bonnie wrote."

"Bonnie wrote it," he qualified. "I just told it to her."

"Well, thank you. It was very…decent of you."

"Look," he retorted, "nobody's worried about being 'decent.' You earned it, that's all. Fair is fair. A. J. Clayburn ain't beholden to anyone."

"Beholden?" Blood abruptly pounded in Jacquelyn's temples. "I get it. You were afraid I'd gloat about the rescue, hold it over you? A mere slip of a greenhorn girl, saving A. J. Clayburn's celebrity butt."

"I admit it," he returned. "You *would* gloat. Now we're even."

"You insufferable, self-loving egotist." She fumed.

"You uppity, conceited snot." He punched right back.

Several minutes passed in awkward silence. Jacquelyn listened to the rattle of the tug chains, the clip-clop of Rip's shod hooves on the blacktop pavement.

Despite her seething anger, she was struck by something he'd just said. *You earned it.* Hazel had reminded her of the same point just minutes earlier. Jacquelyn had indeed ridden McCallum's Trace and survived. Ice princess or not, loser in love or not, she *did* it.

Hazel's original claim sank in again—the trip had changed Jacquelyn. She'd survived much of what the legendary Jake McCallum survived plus some dangers of her own. She had entered the crucible of her own fears and doubts, and she had emerged. Sure, she was bound to see A.J. around Mystery, perhaps even bound to yearn for him for the rest of her life. But what she had survived up on the mountain would strengthen her. And when she should by chance look again into his eyes, she might one day not feel the pain of love lost, but perhaps gratitude that in this short life, she at least had her moments of true love. She certainly had never had them before with anyone else.

As for right now, right here and now...she aimed a sidelong glance at A.J.'s stony, resentful profile.

There was one more important gesture she must find the courage to make. If not, she'd go mad in the unbearable silence.

She cleared her throat. "A.J.?"

He said nothing.

"A.J.?" she repeated.

"Is there a bone in your throat?" he demanded. "You got something to say, spit it out."

A surge of anger almost coaxed her to leap down from the surrey right there. Instead, she fought down the impulse and said calmly, "We both know that certain...indiscretions occurred during our trip. We can't undo the past. But as this very occasion proves, our paths are bound to cross often in a little town like Mystery. Can't we at least try for a civil peace between us?''

He totally surprised her by becoming even more angry.

"Exactly what," he demanded, the ice of suppressed rage in his voice, "do you mean by *indiscretion?*"

Her surprise and confusion only intensified. "Isn't…isn't that obvious?" she floundered. Her extreme discomfort forced her to a stilted, formal language that she detested even as she used it. "Obviously I'm speaking of our night together. Our liaison."

"'Liaison,'" he repeated, his tone mocking the word.

"Yes," she struggled, "but in many ways it was a memorable trip. And if we could simply somehow put that one mistake behind us, then perhaps we could retain a warm acquaintance for the future." My God, she upbraided herself. Are you talking to a man you slept with and love, or are you preparing for law school?

As for A.J., his direct, gunmetal scrutiny held her for an interminable time. Then, in a slow, harsh, almost chilling voice, he spoke.

"For me, what happened between us was no mistake. Unlike you, I slept with you and don't regret it. And after what I felt—what you *made* me feel for you up there on that mountain—I'll be damned if I'll settle for some puny 'warm acquaintance.' I'd rather be dead to you than spend the rest of my life making small talk to a woman I love."

A woman I love.

The shock of those words struck her like blows. A sudden rush of powerful feelings closed her throat before she could say anything.

A.J., clearly starting to feel the sting of this latest humiliation, added bitterly, "One more thing before I shut up. What I felt with you…what I mean is, the kind of people I come from put plenty of meaning into a man and woman connecting like I *thought* we did. If you can seriously just call it a 'mistake,' treat it like nothing, maybe you oughta think about living some other place. Because that's not the kind of people we are in Mystery.''

Now it was Jacquelyn's turn to stare, her eyes filling with unshed tears. There was so much she wanted to say to him right then, so many things he didn't understand, that he misperceived. But her feelings, at this sudden revelation of his own closely guarded emotions, overwhelmed her ability to speak.

The surrey reached the outskirts of town and bore down on the well-lit common square a few blocks ahead of them. Her inability to answer right away was damning her, but she was unable to muster the words that were blossoming in her heart.

"Aw, hell!" he exclaimed, reining in the gelding. The surrey stopped in the middle of deserted Main Street.

"Not even for Hazel, not this time," he said in a quiet, determined voice. "A man's got his pride, after all."

He tipped his hat at Jacquelyn. "You're on your own from here," he told her. "I'm going home and getting drunk."

The surrey swayed as A.J. started to swing down. Devastated, Jacquelyn struggled to find her voice.

"A.J.," she called, barely managing to speak above a whisper. "Those nights had meaning for me, too."

He stopped, then turned around and walked slowly back. He came up on her side of the surrey, only inches from her.

"Speak up," he demanded.

"I said," she replied evenly, "those nights had meaning for me, too."

"That right?" he said, needling her, lifting a sardonic eyebrow. "And just what meaning was that?"

In a low, rough voice, she answered with the only word she could manage. "Love."

Her insides breaking like thin ice, she sat in the surrey, not able to move. Her only instinct at the moment was to salvage any pride she possibly might have left. But she couldn't. She couldn't be an ice princess around him. She just couldn't.

A surprised groan came from A.J.'s throat when her words struck home. His muscular arms enfolded her and pulled her down from the seat, stroking her cheek with a warm hand.

"You know what?" he said tenderly, once he had her in his embrace. "You just said the one word I've been praying to hear from you."

She met his gaze, hardly able to believe that he, too, could feel the kind of loneliness and despair she carried inside. And hardly able to believe that the night on Bridger's Summit and the night afterward were also a cruel always-out-of-reach balm for his soul, too.

"Guess we better finish this ride if we're going to?" he suggested reluctantly.

She nodded, tears in her smile. "Let's knock 'em dead, Jake."

But as the surrey neared the corner of the courthouse, the realization of what had just passed between them seemed to have struck both of them. Despite good intentions, A.J. seemed to forget the horse and surrey and the big crowd waiting for them only seconds away.

He leaned close, taking her hungry lips in a passionate kiss just as Rip came wheeling around the corner into an explosion of lights.

Only the sustained cheering and applause of the assembled townies finally startled the two lovers back into the present moment.

Jacquelyn scooted back over to her side of the seat, but it was too late. The passionate and highly public kiss had just officially opened the festivities on a high note. And there, watching from her place of honor on a wooden viewing stand, stood Hazel, her gnarled hands clutched in glee.

At long last, thought the Matriarch of Mystery, she'd found a way to save her beloved town.

And save it she would.

For this was just the beginning....

Epilogue

From the Helena, Montana *Register*

Mystery, Montana—Rodeo star A. J. Clayburn and noted journalist Jacquelyn Rousseaux exchanged nuptials today at Hazel McCallum's world-famous Lazy M Ranch in Mystery Valley.

A lengthy guest list mingled "old money" Southern aristocrats with celebrities from the international rodeo circuit. As Bonnie Lofton, editor of Mystery's local newspaper put it: "For every pair of Gucci open weaves, I spotted a pair of cowhide boots."

The groom, thirty-one, recently overcame a serious injury to capture his second consecutive World Cup in saddle-bronc riding. His bride, twenty-five, drew national mention earlier this year from the prestigious School of Journalism at Columbia University. Her Montana feature story, "Riding McCallum's Trace," received a Golden Quill Award for excellence in regional reporting.

"I was pleased, but completely surprised, to learn of the romance," Hazel McCallum told reporters. "I'm sure it must have been love at first sight, just spontaneous. And I suspect there's going to be a rash of matrimonies coming up in Mystery."

When asked how she could possibly know that, the cattle baroness only replied with a mysterious smile, "Oh, a woman of my age knows these things."

*　*　*　*　*

When Constance Adams
met up with George Henning,
aka Assistant U.S. Attorney,
Quinn Loudon, little did she suspect
that her life—and her heart—would
never be the same again.

Here's a sneak peek at
THE LAWMAN MEETS HIS BRIDE—

Meagan McKinney's next book
in her riveting series
MATCHED IN MONTANTA,

available only from Silhouette's
Intimate Moments, on sale fall 2000.

I'll let the machine take it, Constance Adams resolved when the telephone chirred at 5:05 p.m.

After all, the business day was over. And she had been on the go, virtually nonstop, showing homes since 11 a.m. This summer it seemed as if every upwardly mobile family east of the Mississippi was clamoring for a vacation home in Mystery, Montana.

It had been a long day of smiles and small talk, and she was tired. Ginny, her assistant, had already gone home, and Constance was on the verge of locking up the office when the phone rang.

Nonetheless, something oddly insistent about the sound, or perhaps it was only her efficient nature, made her pick up before the answering machine could click on.

"Mystery Valley Real Estate," she answered. "This is Constance Adams speaking."

"Yes, Miss Adams, I'm sure glad I caught you."

Her first impression was confusing. The male voice was

seductive, yet sounded impatient and curiously...strained, she decided.

"My name is George Henning," the voice continued, and she recognized a trace of a Northeast accent in the vowels. "I wonder if it would be possible to have a quick look at one of your listings?"

"Of course, Mr. Henning. If you'll just tell me what time is convenient for—"

"No, I mean have a look right now. You see, I'm quite pressed for time. I need to catch a plane later, yet this cabin has just caught my eye. I like it."

"Cabin?" Constance repeated, somewhat surprised. "You must mean the place at the end of the Old Mill Road."

"Yes, that's the one."

She hesitated, her surprise tinged by exasperation. The Old Mill Road cabin was her listing, all right. One of Hazel McCallum's properties. And while it was a quaint, rusting hideaway in the mountains, it hardly represented a fat commission. It was a little too remote, a little too basic, for most of her clients. Still...she hadn't exactly been swamped with offers.

"Well, Mr. Henning, it is rather late. I mean, it would take me some time to drive up into the mountains from here. May I ask—where are you right now?"

"In front of the cabin, actually. Saw your name on the sign. I called on my cell phone."

"Oh, I see."

A cell phone, she thought. Yes, maybe that explained the curious sound to his voice. At any rate, she simply should have said no, not today. But something about his urgency compelled her to hesitate, and he allowed her no time to harden her resolve.

"I know it's late, Miss Adams, and I do apologize for the inconvenience. But I really am pressed for time. This place looks fine from the outside. A quick peek at the interior, and maybe we could reach terms today?"

She frowned slightly, and a skeptical dimple appeared at one corner of her expressive lips. The caller sounded intelligent and well-spoken. Yet the urgency in his tone puzzled her—perhaps even worried her a bit.

Inexplicably, however, she found herself giving in.

"All right, Mr. Henning, since you're in a hurry. I'll leave right now. I should be there in about forty minutes."

The moment she hung up, however, Constance realized what a stupid thing she had just agreed to do: meet a stranger, as night came on, way up on a God-forgotten slope of the Rocky Mountains.

She almost called him back to cancel. But if he was catching a plane later, she reasoned, then maybe she was tossing a sale right down a rat hole. The cabin was no hot-ticket item, she reminded herself. The female in her was nervous, but the business person in her won the brief debate.

So she settled on a common-sense compromise. She quickly dialed her parents' number. With the size of her family, there was usually no problem catching someone. Since the cabin was in a remote area, at least someone would know where she was. Thank goodness for cell phones....

COMING NEXT MONTH

#1303 BACHELOR DOCTOR—Barbara Boswell
Man of the Month
He was brilliant, handsome—and couldn't keep his mind off nurse
Callie Sheely! No one had ever captured Dr. Trey Weldon's attention
like Callie, but she insisted their relationship would never work. Could
Trey convince Callie otherwise with a soul-stirring seduction…?

#1304 MIDNIGHT FANTASY—Ann Major
Body & Soul
Tag rescued Claire when she was in dire peril—and then showed her
the delights of true fantasy. Could this very real man of her dreams
save Claire from even greater danger—marriage to the wrong man?

#1305 WIFE FOR HIRE—Amy J. Fetzer
Wife, Inc.
What horse breeder Nash Rayburn needed was a temporary wife. What
he got was Hayley Albright, his former lover and soon-to-be doctor.
But Hayley still carried a torch for Nash. Could she rekindle *his* love—
this time permanently?

#1306 RIDE A WILD HEART—Peggy Moreland
Texas Grooms
Bronc rider Pete Dugan always knew that he was not cut out to be a
family man—then Carol Benson walked back into his life. Carol had
commitment written all over her, but when she revealed her long-held
secret, would Pete be ready to say "I do"?

#1307 BLOOD BROTHERS—Anne McAllister and Lucy Gordon
2-in-1 Original Stories
Double trouble! That's what you got when cousins Montana cowboy
Gabe McBride and British lord Randall Stanton traded places. What
Gabe and Randall got was the challenge of their lives—wooing the
women of their hearts. Because to win Claire McBride and Frederika
Crossman, these two blood brothers would need to exert all their
British pluck and cowboy try!

#1308 COWBOY FOR KEEPS—Kristi Gold
Single mom Dana Landry cared only about catering to the special
needs of her daughter. Then cowboy Will Baker taught Dana she had
to take care of *her* needs, as well—and he was just the man to help.
But when the night was over, would Will still want to be Dana's
cowboy for keeps?

CMN0600

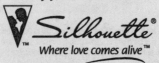

"Take Your Boots Off," AJ Demanded. "Then Crawl Inside My Sleeping Bag.

"We're going to pool our warmth."

Jacquelyn started to shake her head.

"Look," he insisted, "believe me, I'm not making a pass at you. When I do that, I don't bother with tricks. But we could be in this cavern for some time yet, and you're not freezing to death on my watch. Now stow the modesty and crawl in here."

"Fine," she snapped as she wiggled into the sleeping bag. "Besides, we've got a dozen layers of clothing between us."

Already she was warmer. But he was so close. And so was the scent of him—dark, male and enticing. Dangerous....

Dear Reader,

Silhouette is celebrating its 20th anniversary throughout 2000! So, to usher in the first summer of the millennium, why not indulge yourself with six powerful, passionate, provocative love stories from Silhouette Desire?

Jackie Merritt returns to Desire with a MAN OF THE MONTH who's *Tough To Tame*. Enjoy the sparks that fly between a rugged ranch manager and the feisty lady who turns his world upside down! Another wonderful romance from RITA Award winner Caroline Cross is in store for you this month with *The Rancher and the Nanny*, in which a rags-to-riches hero learns trust and love from the riches-to-rags woman who cares for his secret child.

Watch for Meagan McKinney's *The Cowboy Meets His Match*—an octogenarian matchmaker sets up an ice-princess heiress with a virile rodeo star. The Desire theme promotion THE BABY BANK, about sperm-bank client heroines who find love unexpectedly, concludes with Susan Crosby's *The Baby Gift*. Wonderful newcomer Sheri WhiteFeather offers another irresistible Native American hero with *Cheyenne Dad*. And Kate Little's hero reunites with his lost love in a marriage of convenience to save her from financial ruin in *The Determined Groom*.

So come join in the celebration and start your summer off on the supersensual side—by reading all six of these tantalizing Desire books!

Enjoy!

Joan Marlow Golan

Joan Marlow Golan
Senior Editor, Silhouette Desire

Please address questions and book requests to:
Silhouette Reader Service
U.S.: 3010 Walden Ave., P.O. Box 1325, Buffalo, NY 14269
Canadian: P.O. Box 609, Fort Erie, Ont. L2A 5X3